MOUSE
ON THE
MOUNTAIN

PAUL BRYAN

Brilliant Books Literary
137 Forest Park Lane Thomasville
North Carolina 27360 USA

CONTENTS

You will know him when he comes,
Scampering like the sun across the sky,
An enemy to all Blues and Bums,
The mighty, mighty Mouse on high.

All hail the Mouse on the Mountain,
The mighty, mighty Mouse on high.

-Shimnon the Elder

PROLOGUE

I was there for the birth of our democracy. I witnessed the miraculous evolution of a perfect form of Government. It all began with the division from the Reds and the discovery of a new land in which to grow and multiply and prosper, and it was all premised on the radical notion of freedom to think about things that did not ultimately matter. Of course, things that did not ultimately matter were deadly serious matters to us, and that indeed is what compelled us to create our fatherland.

Some of us believed that One Paw was the only sacred being in the universe; others maintained that One Eye was superior to all other beings; and yet still others, in an effort to get attention and be contentious, asserted that One Paw did not really exist and that, moreover, One Eye was nothing more than an illusion. If you were still not certain where to stand on these issues, fortunately there was a place for you also in this, our glorious new country, as one of the Undecided. The point, however, which I set out to make in this paragraph was simply this: that because none of us could agree on the many and diverse ways of thinking about things that did not ultimately matter, we simply agreed to disagree. Freedom of opinion is what founded our nation, a nation of disgruntled, frequently antagonistic Mice.

It was clear to me and to all of my comrades that our form of democracy was far better than the monarchy of the Reds. I hesitate to cast epithets, and I personally try not to prejudice myself against any system that is different from our Government (for I *was* educated in a liberal arts college), but only a complete moron would not see that our country was invincible, and only an even more complete idiot would not see how it got to be that way.

Our country was founded on the notion that expansion was not only profitable but also inexorable, and would no doubt continue forever in this massive stretch of land between the Two Rivers. Over the last ten years, we had grown and grown, until today—*just look at us!* What started out a meager, struggling colony had, over the course of time, developed into a substantial gathering of Mice. The food was plentiful, the jobs were bounteous, the economy booming, the military powerful.

Growth was inevitable.

Our President, at the time when this history begins, was a Mouse by the name of Oliver—we did have a President, as well as a complicated scheme of checks and balances, with a legislative and a judicial system. He was of the free opinion that Bummunism, an economic and philosophical way of life for the Blues, a large group of Mice several fields across the East River, was not only morally inferior to Infinite Expansionalism, but also deprived Mice of all their One Paw-given rights—namely, the right to get what one deserves in life without becoming enslaved to the Collective.

These two systems—Bummunism and Infinite Expansionalism—were the two primary forms of Government in existence and could not have been more diverse in their separate principles. I shall discuss them more in depth later.

For now, be content in knowing that I am an Historian, a Green Mouse twelve-years-old, who once lived contentedly between the Rivers in a land we called, not without some measure of pride in regard of our heroic past, Sunflower Country.

TO THE SENATE BURROW

In my old age, I found that I was usually awake even before the crack of dawn. I used to bustle about in the dark trying to think what the day ahead might hold, perhaps munching on a few sunflower kernels. Without a fireplace, I confess, it did get a little cold in the winter, but at least I had my set of matches and could light one at my convenience to warm my claws, while my fellow citizens had to do without. I had learned that the amenities of the rich were reserved for the rich with good reason. The logic of it all I had no need to question.

However, I was content with my knowledge. The world would continue revolving with or without the rich and the poor, and a demarcation based on the economy no longer interested me; for, you see, I had been an Historian for ten long years, ever since the birth of our Sunflower Country. I had been exposed to every idea, every bias, every justification the world has to offer, and I had been lulled to sleep by the monotony of my country's success.

On that morning so long ago, shortly before sunrise, Niner paid me a visit. He was almost as old as I, and of the opinion that the aged must stick together, else lose their rights. Niner was a great friend of mine and had been for a very long time, but his opinions strayed far beyond common sense, and at times I found myself losing all patience with the poor Mouse.

"Percy," he said, as he entered my burrow. "The sun is almost up, Percy. It's time to go to work."

"Yes, Niner."

"By the way, I hear the latest issue in Congress is Female rights. It seems the issue of Abortion has once again hit center stage. What will the Government do about it? Take away individual rights, or sacrifice future lives?"

"I see you've had your cup of Alertness Elixir this morning," I remarked sarcastically. The issue of Mouse Abortion had disgusted me for a very long time, and during the past couple of days the Senate had engaged in a heated debate about it, which further disgusted me. I made no additional effort to reply.

"But you haven't answered my question," continued Niner. "Is Mouse Abortion right or wrong, and what will be the Senate's ruling on the matter?"

"It's all opinion. Opinion, opinion, opinion," I droned, not quite fully awake.

"It would seem," said Niner, "that a Female Mouse has the right to use her body in any way she wishes. Who are we to question a One Paw-given right?"

This country had disintegrated into the land of rights and wills— the right to do this and not do that, the will to live, the will to die, the right to have inalienable rights. Rights, rights, rights. It got to be truly annoying the more you thought about it. I often found myself wondering if there were any escape from the tension of the world.

"I am not terribly interested in your arguments this morning, Niner. Just look outside," I gestured with my claw. "Already the sun peeks over the trees at us. One Paw has truly blessed the Greens in Sunflower Country today."

I failed to mention earlier that I was a rather distinguished citizen, not just an Historian, but a Senator as well, one of only five in all. I had accumulated over many years a reputation for dependability, a reputation for steadfastness in times of confusion, and finally, a reputation for generosity to those around me. My standing with the community was benevolent and positive. In everything I did, the Mice of my country came first.

I was the perfect politician.

Every word that passed by my lips was perfectly pronounced, with just the right accent and just the proper amount of air being manipulated in its flow past the tongue. All of my thoughts were guided by the rigorous discipline of reason. In my line of work, it paid to be levelheaded.

Niner persisted in his curiosity, if only for a moment: "Anyhow, as I was saying, it is my sincere opinion that a Mousette should have the right to do whatever she so desires with her body—it is, after all, her body, not yours or mine—speaking of which, I have not been exercising as much as I ought recently, and as a dread consequence, my own body has wilted while my mind has blossomed. What do you think of that, Percy? What do you think of that, eh?"

"You speak in circles, as usual, Niner." Sometimes it was better to ignore what the poor old Mouse said because, more often than not, he was spouting a heap of irrational gibberish that not even the most sympathetic of minds could make sense of. I made a bid to change the subject: "Let's have Alertness Elixir on the porch and watch as the sun ascends over the tree-line, what say?"

"A splendid idea!" he agreed.

When we were comfortably seated in our mounds of cedar shavings with mugs of Alertness Elixir in paw, Niner proposed something unexpected, which took me utterly by surprise considering all the rubbish he had babbled before.

"When are you going to run for President, Percy?"

I nearly choked on my drink at this, an outrageous suggestion to say the least. "Well," I began, once fully recovered, "I do not think that I shall ever be President of Sunflower Country. I am more than happy as a Senator for now. Who could possibly ask for more? I remain in good—rather, I should say *excellent*—standing with the Mice of my district, and the thought of jeopardizing such good fortune by overreaching my grasp does not suit to me at all. Not one tiny bit."

"You are a crazy Mouse not to use your leverage, Percy, to get more than you currently have. The Presidency is certainly within your grasp."

"Who thinks so?" I queried, suspecting that Niner now spoke for someone else, not just for himself.

"Oh, I should say all the good Mice of your district, not to mention a hoard of Mice far and wide, would support your decision to make a push. And better now than never, if you ask me. The election is only a month away—speaking of which, I need to visit the dentist next month as well, on the third if I am not mistaken. What do you think of that, Percy? What do you think of that, eh?"

"I think you are just being silly," I asserted with all the confidence of a true psychologist. "And besides, it is about time to get ready to go to work. As you can see, the sun is now well above the tree-line."

I said goodbye to Niner. I would not see him again until the following morning. A tangled mass of political matters weighed heavily upon my shoulders. That day, we would determine whether or not to pass a bill which would prohibit the ownership of lethal Arsenic, a deadly substance that, although good for warding off burglars, nevertheless had been misused in the past, leading to several accidental and unwelcome murders. The issue came hot on the heels of the Mouse Abortion argument, which I have already said disgusted me to no end, and would no doubt spark heated debates and controversy. I looked forward to the challenge.

I dressed in my uniform—suit and tie—a descendant of ridiculous Victorian costumes which I have always found uncomfortable on my animal skin, and began the long hike into the city to join my comrades. Our job was the most crucial in all of the country, for we proposed and passed laws that had an effect on everyone.

Representation was terribly important. We operated under the logical assumption that large groups of Mice could be represented by a single Mouse. This seemed a bit problematic to me the more I thought about it, but for that reason alone, I tried not to think about it. Suffice it to say, I was not able to voice all the concerns of the Mice I represented; however, it was never outside the realm of possibility that I could voice a few of their concerns, here and there, when they agreed with my fancy—all told, probably about one percent. But this did not seem to worry the Mice, who were happy in their ignorance and namelessness. Besides, it was by far the most efficient system of Government ever invented by Mousekind.

As I walked the distance to the Senate Burrow, an establishment constructed of twigs and grasses and a half-hollowed out log that came about as the result of a tree falling in a storm many years ago, I tried not to think of all the problems which had to be resolved in our country. The further one thought on it, the more one tended to realize that, although there may be solutions to these problems, the solutions themselves merely begat further problems requiring further solutions. If I hadn't known any better, I would have been forced to conclude that the workings of Government and Mouse were really quite cyclical.

I passed by a large crowd of young Mice on my right, who were apparently college students taking a break from the tedium of their work to listen to a performer, whose name was, I believe, Twister, as he made the most One Paw-awful noises a Mouse ever heard. The kids seemed pleased for whatever it was worth, jumping up and down and jiggling their bodies without any direction or coordination. I shook my head in what could only have been contempt and scurried on towards my destination.

When at last I arrived, I was greeted outside by two other Mice, whose names were Teddy and Bobby. They accosted me eagerly, and thus the early morning conversation commenced.

"Good morning, Percy!" both squealed at once.

"Good morning!" I responded, matching their silly enthusiasm.

"Which way will you be voting today," asked Teddy, "for or against Mouse Abortion?"

"I thought we voted on that yesterday," I replied sarcastically.

"No, we never voted. We just discussed it. Remember?"

"Then in that case, I shall vote against."

"Ahhh!" I watched as the two of them reeled backwards and huddled together, clearly stunned by what I had said. Teddy and Bobby had a reputation in the Senate for being excessively liberal in their perspectives. Of the remaining three, two were fanatically conservative—their names were Chipper and Harold—and I myself walked the middle line, capable of being swayed by good argument one way or the other. As you can imagine, my vote was pivotal in almost all the issues we discussed.

They returned with a veritable volley of reproach.

"How could you vote against a Female Mouse's inalienable right to do with her body as she wishes?"

"Haven't you heard the fiddler metaphor?"

"Where are your good wits about you, Percy? Don't you see that if you deny a Female Mouse the right to an Abortion, she will be unable to dispose of unwanted pregnancies?"

"If a Mousette has a fiddler crab attached to her back—"

"Enough! Enough! Enough!" I brought their incessant babbling to a halt. "I have heard all of the arguments."

"Then explain where you stand on this dreadfully important issue," Bobby intoned.

"First of all, the fiddler crab argument doesn't hold water. If a Female Mouse is allowed to do whatever she wishes to her body, then we might as well allow her to jump off Mount Enex with haywire wrapped around her fragile neck. Besides, who has the authority to determine that multiple embryos are, in point of fact, a part of her body? Granted, they are dependant on her for survival, but does that mean they belong to her body?

"Abortion comes down to just one simple fact—it may not be murder in actuality, but it is certainly murder in potentiality. Once the egg and sperm unite, the chances of life are greatly increased. It is wrong, in my opinion, to snuff out what has about an eighty-five percent chance of growing into a living, breathing, thinking Mouse if given proper nourishment and time."

I stopped when I realized their jaws had gone slack and they were staring at me in utter disbelief.

"What do you mean, *potentiality*? If murder is not murder in actuality, it is not murder, plain and simple!" Teddy retorted.

"Opinions, opinions," I said. "You have yours. I have mine. I refuse to engage further in such a petty argument with you this morning. Now, if you will excuse me."

"You will lose all the Female Mouse votes in your district!" cried Bobby, in vain.

This did not concern me, for I was old and planning to retire soon anyhow. Brushing past the two stunned creatures, I made my way into the Senate Burrow and took my seat. Bobby and Teddy followed me in and assumed their places in the cedar shavings opposite me. We had pilfered a local Carpenter-Man's shop for the material to make our comfortable bedding.

"Percy," began Bobby, bringing up the horrible subject once more, "we urge you to reconsider. The vote will be cast this morning, before all discussion about Arsenic Rights begins. We need your vote. We are desperate."

"Did you know," said Teddy, in an attempt to magnify his political clout, "that I won a spelling contest when I was in the third grade?"

"That's nothing," said Bobby, "I won an award as the fastest Mouse in my grade when I was just two years old."

"Well, so what? Were you considered the smartest Mouse in all of Sunflower Country by age five?"

"Of course not, but I was strongest by age four!"

This ridiculous contest, which was not at all uncommon among Mice of extraordinary political stature, might have continued had I not seen the wisdom to intervene and, yet again, bring their incessant babbling to a halt. "Enough of this nonsense!" I cried. "I am ready to get out of politics altogether."

"Even if you stood a tolerable chance at becoming President next year?"

"Well," I began, somewhat dubiously. "I'm not so sure about that." I was flattered for the second time that day, and this flattery had supplied my ego with enough conceitedness that I felt it was ready to burst from all the pressure.

"You jest with us!"

"I am too old and tired to jest with anyone."

The two Mice turned away from me as Chipper, who was three years younger than I, brought the gavel down and called the assembly to order. "Order, order, order! This meeting of the Senate has now been called to order. As you know, we must get a vote this morning on Mouse Abortion—whether to permit or prohibit it—and then later we shall have to discuss Arsenic Rights.

First, let us take the vote. Indicate either yes or no, by chirping either 'Yea' or 'Nay,' whether you are for or against Mouse Abortion when your name is called. A single scratch will be put on the bark for every single vote."

"Harold?"

"Nay."

"Bobby?"

"Yea."

"Teddy?"

"Yea."

"Percy?"

"Nay."

"And I, Chipper, vote 'Nay' as well. That makes for three scratches against, and two for. The majority is against Mouse Abortion, therefore, from this day forth, it is outlawed—"

"Wait!" I interrupted him, surprising myself with the strength of my voice. "Don't you all think it would be a bit silly to outlaw something so prevalent and so apparently necessary in our society. I admit, I am wholly against the ideology of Mouse Abortion. The practice seems outright immoral to me. But it would be folly to try and prohibit something of this magnitude. Haven't we tried something like this before—the prohibition of fermented corn juice—and didn't it backfire in our faces? It seems to me we are not dealing with an entirely Government issue here. If we try to prohibit, we shall almost certainly fail, and many Mice will be hurt along the way. The best course of action to take, therefore, is none at all. Let the public know where we stand on the issue, and perhaps our reputation may carry some weight in the community. But I repeat: prohibition is utter folly and will backfire in our faces the way fermented corn juice did. The Government should not poke its nose in things it has no control over. To even discuss Mouse Abortion in the workings of Government is a ridiculous waste of time."

When I finished, the members of the Senate fell quiet for what seemed like an eternity. I noticed that Chipper was staring at me with a good deal of disgust apparent in his facial expression, as if to say, 'How dare you think that!' I waited and waited, but nobody said a word. I looked around and saw that everyone was staring at me— Bobby and Teddy with expressions of absolute perplexity, Harold with amused curiosity. Chipper looked as if he wanted to kill.

"Well, I never—" began Chipper, breaking the silence before he was interrupted.

"Percy's got a point!" Bobby practically yelled at the top of his lungs.

"Indeed!" Teddy concurred.

"Of course *you two* would agree with him," said Chipper, who by then was thoroughly disheartened.

"I myself am adamantly opposed to Mouse Abortion and would be more than happy if this abominable crime carried with it the penalty of death," said Harold. "My feelings aside, however, we should probably put this to a vote, whether to take action or not on the issue of Mouse Abortion in consideration of Percy's opinion that it would be futile to do so."

Chipper looked around him, pausing to lock eyes with each of us. It was apparent to him that we were all conspiring against him.

At last, however, he was forced to relent in his stubborn disposition. Maintaining his dignity, he spoke: "Oh, very well. But this time I abstain from voting, which is what I should've done the first time. I have a personal vested interest in the matter; for, you see, my niece had a Mouse Abortion two years ago against the wishes of her family."

"We hold nothing against you, Chipper," said Harold.

Chipper continued. "If there are no further objections, we shall now put this to a vote. If you favor not taking action on Mouse Abortion, say 'Yea,' otherwise say 'Nay.' A single scratch will be put on the bark for every single vote."

"Harold?"

"A reluctant yea."

"Bobby?"

"Yea."

"Teddy?"

"Yea."

"Percy?"

"Yea."

"Then, as I abstain from the voting, it is agreed that we shall not take action on the issue of Mouse Abortion. And that concludes that. Now it is time for other weighty matters, matters that have a grave impact on all the Mice of our country. The issue to which I am currently referring is simply this—Arsenic Control. Should a Mouse, according to his Constitutional rights, be allowed to bear Arsenic, or should we pass into law a clause prohibiting ownership of the poison in any way, shape or form?"

"Who are you to decide?" barked a Mouse by the name of Luke, who had just stepped into the hall. He was followed by several Mice, what seemed a hundred in all, who each had a special interest in the outcome of this debate.

"Bearing Arsenic is a Constitutional and a One Paw-given right!" shouted another. "You can't take that away from us!"

Another faction of Mice filed in through the other door and immediately began pointing fingers and calling their adversaries "Murderers!"

Numerous *Amen*'s and concurrences followed. A scuffle broke out on the floor. I realized for the first time just how serious the issue was and determined, according to the dictum of wisdom, to avoid coming down heavily on one side or the other; for where one makes a decision in life, one always eliminates a possibility, and to eliminate either of the two possibilities at stake here would be to incur the wrath of a great many already angry Mice.

"Order, order, order! This meeting of the Senate has now been called to order! If you cannot cooperate and hold your peace, you will be compelled to leave the premises by the Sunflower Country Police!"

Chipper then turned to Harold, "Speaking of which, where are the Sunflower Country Police?"

"I shall summon them," said Harold, and he was off on his errand.

The crowd grew increasingly restless. Clawtips were pointed accusingly and volatile words were exchanged on both sides. Somebody picked up a pawful of cedar and tossed it in another Mouse's face. Before long a riot seemed unavoidable. The point of no return was fast approaching.

Just at that moment, to the great fortune of everyone present, the Police showed up in full force—a collection of the most physically gifted and athletic, though for the most part senseless, Mice in the entire country. And at last it seemed everything would be calm again.

"This session is now called to order," said Chipper, "and for the last time, I hope."

Harold was back in his seat, and we all sat eagerly awaiting the leader of the Senate's call to begin.

"We shall begin by hearing the argument from both sides. You, the Mice of this country faithful enough in the workings of Government and democracy to show up here today to voice your opinions—you will pick one among you, one for each side, to make a short statement regarding your position. These statements will be heard and acknowledged by the Senate and will be closely regarded in the making of our decision on the matter. Am I understood?"

"Yes!" returned a chorus of voices.

"Then be proud of your Mousehood and take a stand, one way or the other. Let us hear from the side in favor of Arsenic possession first. Who among you will be SpokesMouse?"

A large, burly Mouse stepped forward and bowed, his nose very nearly touching the ground as he did so. "I am Rocky," he began, "and I am speaking on behalf of the rights of common citizens to bear Arsenic." The audience fell into silence.

"First of all, the right to bear Arsenic is a One Paw-given right and a Constitutional right. As such, it cannot be taken away from us without first altering the Constitution with an amendment. But what we have to realize is this: our forefathers first put that clause into the Constitution for a very good reason—namely, for individual protection against outer hostilities. If a Mouse feels threatened in any way and is unable to protect himself physically, it is his One Paw-given right to be able to defend himself with Arsenic. What, for example, is my grandmother supposed to do if she is assaulted at night by a bunch of young hooligans? If your proposal to ban Arsenic goes through, she will not be able to defend herself and she will have to die. This is not just. Everyone among you knows of at least one Mouse who could profit from Arsenic. I urge you therefore to consider the evil consequences of voting to ban Arsenic, and to reconsider all the many advantages and benefits to be derived from its ownership. Be wise and just. Be strong and smart. Vote sensibly. Vote honestly. Vote 'Yea' to Arsenic. That is all I have to say."

Half the assembly began clapping and hooting joyfully. The other half glared furiously across the room at them. Arsenic Rights was a serious matter indeed.

Some of the Senators nodded tiredly, having been audience to more than a thousand excitable speeches in their lives.

Suddenly, Chipper brought an end to the jubilation: "Now let us hear from the side which is opposed to the possession of Arsenic. Who among you will be SpokesMouse? Step forth, and be proud of your Mousehood."

A small, svelte Mouse stepped forward and bowed daintily, her nose very nearly touching the ground as she did so. "I am Pepper," she began, "and I am speaking in opposition to the rights of common citizens to bear Arsenic." The audience fell into silence.

"It is our sincere opinion that if common citizens are allowed to bear Arsenic, they will do far more harm than good. We have a riddled history of this particular problem, that Mice of the community have misused Arsenic and have accidentally, as it were, killed other Mice and destroyed the lives of close, loved ones and family members. This is a serious dilemma for Sunflower Country—whether to take away Arsenic Rights. My colleagues and I are opposed to Arsenic Rights, which are all too often abused, and will fight for the legislation against the right to bear Arsenic until the day we die. Perhaps in such a violent state as ours, we shall all perish to the dreaded Arsenic before the appropriate legislation is passed. I personally lost a cousin and an uncle to unlawful use of the poison, and I do not intend to lose any more of my family simply because the rest of the country is too hypocritical to recognize the deleterious effects of this Manmade demon. May the demon be buried forever. May innocent Mice live to tell their stories another day. May we all rest in peace. Vote no to Arsenic. That is all I have to say."

After much jubilation on the other side, and several weary yawns from the Senators themselves, Chipper broke in once again to restore order to the Senate Burrow. "The Mice of our country have voiced their separate and divergent opinions regarding the matter of Arsenic Rights. It is now up to us, the individual members of the Senate, to take these respectable opinions into consideration, and cast a vote, either for or against Arsenic Rights, thus transforming them into law. The audience will remain silent until such time as a decision has been made."

"We shall begin with you, Harold. What is your opinion?"

"I am in favor of Arsenic Rights primarily because it is a Constitutional right to bear Arsenic, and we do not have the authority to take that away from the Mice of this country without going against our forefathers' best judgment."

"Very well. That makes for one vote in favor of the right to bear Arsenic. Bobby, where do you stand?"

"I am opposed to Arsenic Rights because I don't trust the Mice of this country to use this poison sensibly. In the past, it has been misused. You cannot change Mice. Some of them are evil. Others, good. How far are we willing to trust them to carry around a substance as deadly as Arsenic?"

"That's one for and one against. Teddy, what do you think about this?"

"I am also opposed, and for reasons very similar to Bobby's. We have trusted the good Mice of our country time and time again, and repeatedly they have mishandled and abused their rights. If the violence of Mice must go unchecked, then the liberty to bear Arsenic, granted to us by One Paw above, must necessarily be curbed."

"That's one for and two against. Percy, what are your thoughts on the matter?"

I paused dramatically before commencing with my speech, which was by now thoroughly rehearsed in my head. A hushed awe fell across the crowd. I could literally feel the energy sifting in the air. I turned to face the Mice, some from my district, all from my country, and gradually began a process I like to refer to as political exploitation. The words flowed out of me effortlessly.

"I cast my vote in opposition to my fellow Senators, and call thereby for a compromise on this dreadfully important issue. I am in favor of the right to bear Arsenic among good, upstanding citizens of this country, or among adults who have proven themselves more than worthy. I am opposed, however, to the right to bear Arsenic among criminals, youths, and Mice of unstable background. Therefore, according to the mandates of rigorous logic, I vote that we permit only certain citizens the right to bear this poison. The problem of any accidents arising from the mishandling of Arsenic may thus be circumvented, while yet we may forestall the decision to eradicate all Arsenic Rights. I believe that bearing Arsenic is a Constitutional right that we can ill-afford to vanquish; whereas when the privilege is misused, it can and has rendered many of us miserable. I have considered this long and with great deliberation, and have come to the conclusion that perhaps some wise measure of restraint should be placed on the right to bear Arsenic without taking away individual liberties as they currently stand. To some extent, I vote yea and nay. I vote compromise. This issue needs to be considered in more detail."

I waited for a reaction among my fellow Mice, but for several seconds none seemed forthcoming. Then at last a brave soul started clapping, and, as a trickle gradually builds momentum to become a river raging down the mountain, the whole crowd soon burst into applause. By One Paw, it was more than that! It was a standing ovation, and well deserved. I do not mean to appear the kind of Mouse who always pats himself on the back in that self-congratulatory manner that so many conceited Mice are capable of, but I could not deny the intense pleasure I felt at soaking up all this glory and attention.

Before long a chant began to arise from the congregated Mice: "Percy, Percy, Percy, Percy!" Then this was replaced by the daring postulation, "Percy for President! Percy for President!" which continued for some time before Chipper hammered with his gavel until everybody got quiet.

To be quite frank with you, I was stunned speechless. Fortunately I was not obliged to speak at that time, else for certain I would have tripped over my own tongue. I look back on it now as the very beginning of my grand adventure, the beginning of my ascendancy to the seat of President of Sunflower Country, and the beginning of my understanding of just how valuable my ideas and I were to the Greens of my native land. The remotest possibility of my becoming President had not even been seriously considered until that one rejoicing moment when I received a standing ovation. I had all but determined to retire as a Senator and bid permanent farewell to everything political in life. I had served my country well, and it was time to say goodbye, but the Mice I had grown to respect and love saw it differently. They pictured me as President of the Greens. Outrageous! Apparently my reputation had carried further than even I had imagined was possible.

"Order, order, order! There will be order in this burrow now! The Presidential election is far away, a whole month if I am not mistaken. So whether we like it or not, it is back to the business at paw. What will be the decision on Arsenic control? Harold, have you an opinion?"

"Yes, upon hearing Percy's wise words, I vote that we establish a procedure to determine who is fit, and who unfit, to carry Arsenic. The Mice of this country deserve better treatment. Such a policy would undoubtedly abolish much of the crime that is prevalent in our society."

"I concur," said Bobby.

"As do I," Teddy echoed.

After a long moment in which he appeared to be contemplating how he himself ought to vote, Chipper spoke: "Then it is agreed upon, by not only a majority vote, but a unanimous one, that we, the Mice of Sunflower Country, do hereby propose a law which would regulate the ownership of the lethal substance named by Man and known as Arsenic, and that we would restrict its usage in our beloved land according to individual criminal history and sanity, for the ultimate betterment of all our lives, and for the moral progress of our nation as a whole. One Paw bless you, each and every one!"

The gavel sounded once more before the crowd erupted.

A NEW DEVELOPMENT

As I made my way home that night, I considered for the very first time what being President of Sunflower Country would feel like. I fancied myself escorted around by the Secret Service, making all manner of important decisions for the Republic, and ruling over one thousand discontented Mice. I imagined that, in due time, I could amend all the wrongs of my country and promote our growth past the boundary of the Two Rivers. I would advocate exploration into the great Unknown and nationalistic expansion beyond our current territory. Indeed, the black emptiness of the Northern Frontier was a possibility not to be discounted.

The more I thought on it, the more the idea of "Presidency" agreed with me. For years I had proven that I was a very capable leader in the Senate. The Mice of my country would back me up one hundred percent. Why, just after our meeting today, Rocky, the Mouse who had spoken in favor of Arsenic Rights, came up to me and said: "If you were running for President, Mr. Percy, you could count on having *my* vote!" And then there was Pepper: "Mr. Percy, you are such a fine and eloquent speaker; you are able to devise meaningful compromises in the blink of an eye. I do hope that you will consider running in the upcoming election as President of Sunflower Country. You would certainly have my vote, not to mention most of your district's."

"Yes, yes. It is a possibility I have considered many times," I lied. "I thank you for your honesty, and come November—who knows? Perhaps I shall make a run at it after all."

At home in my burrow I had more time to think about it. Thusly did I come to what was rather obviously the most important decision of my life: whether to step down gracefully from politics and retire with dignity, or to continue into the fire and make one final push for the exalted seat of the Presidency. You, Good Reader, might think it was easy—the answer to this decision, that is—but for the longest time I was utterly lost and profoundly befuddled.

I'm afraid to say—no, on second thought, I am *not* afraid to say—that, in the end, it was my ego that would strengthen my resolve, forming a barrier of granite around my mind with which to ward off all thoughts of ineptitude. I envisioned myself sitting high atop a grand throne, all the power in the world at my clawtips. I imagined myself transmitting clandestine advice to my associates, giving a variety of orders, squeaking rudely at my inferiors, and passing only those bills which agreed with my fancy into law. I saw the future, and it could not have appeared more pleasing and lustrous.

It was all clear to me. Harold would be my Vice President, Chipper would be my Secretary of Defense and primary foreign diplomat. Oh, just look at all I could do for my precious Sunflower Country! We would continue to expand and multiply exponentially, becoming even stronger and more invincible than before, stretching far beyond all known territories and into the dangerous lands outside of our country! All the Mice in the world would adore me, the most gracious leader in history! I would carry on the tradition of my extraordinary ancestors with flawless execution! I would return majesty and nobility to my office!

Considering the possibility of winning, the mere thought of all the obligations that would be placed on me wrinkled my brow. Why, if ever I did fall short of perfection, someone would probably see fit to assassinate me. What if I were unable to protect my country from intruders? What if Snake attacks increased instead of decreased? What if the economy bottomed out on my shift? What if there were some sort of militaristic coup, and I were forcibly deposed from power? These doubts and many more circulated through my brain.

I finally fell to sleep thinking about it—*and dreamt about it even further!* It must have been etched permanently in my sub-consciousness. The idea that I could be President appealed to me more than I cared to admit, but my dreams evolved from bright and wonderful to dark and foreboding. The deeper I fell into sleep, the more disturbing became my nightmare, which consisted more or less of the following:

I woke up with the sun glaring in my eyes through my peephole. Niner was waiting for me, a mug of Alertness Elixir in paw. He said, "Good morning, President Percy! Ah, and what a joyful morning it is!" I would have responded to this bizarre statement, except I was quite literally missing my tongue and could not speak a word. I got out of bed and found that my coordination was faulty and out of line. I hobbled and danced my way clumsily out the front door. To my surprise, there was a large group of Mice congregated outside my hole, and they were all carrying banners and signs that said something to the effect that I was an Anti-Bummunist, and hence ought to be put to death. I hurried past them. Three other Mice escorted me (they were soldiers meant to protect a Mouse in power). Moments later, I was in my office—the office of President of Sunflower

Country—and I saw an unsigned bill on my desk which I could not read, but which I had a premonition was something evil. So I ripped it to shreds with my claws and turned to look out the window, where I saw a huge Snake peering in at me, its fangs dripping poison and its tongue flickering in and out repeatedly. Just at that moment I thought I was going to die, but something lifted me into the air and threw me roughly, whiskers over rump, into a cage. I saw Chipper and Harold in there with me. We were carried by a Man into a vast, clean space with sharp corners and a horrible smell. I watched as the Man picked up Harold and injected him with something from a syringe. Then he did the same to Chipper. For some reason, he left me alone. I stood on my back legs and observed what was going on. First Harold was taken, and I saw the Man cut open his head with a sharp knife, then take a spoon and dig out his brain. "Ah yes, here was a smart one!" he said. "The medicine must have worked beautifully!" I watched as he performed this same procedure on Chipper, first slicing apart the head, then extracting the gray matter with a spoon. I wanted to scream in terror, but nothing came out of my mouth. "Another brilliant specimen! Who knows what this one might have been thinking?" As the Man's hand entered the cage one last time and made as if to reach for me…

I woke up.

The sun was shining directly into my eyes, just as in the dream, but the similarity ended there. I was sweating profusely, and felt like I had been steaming in a pot on a Man's stove for some extraordinary length of time. I turned over onto my stomach and saw that I was not alone. Niner was with me, as were Harold, Chipper, Teddy, and Bobby. A Female Mouse Nurse stood nearby, and another, whom I did not immediately detect, was rubbing my shoulder and saying soothing words into my left ear.

"He's finally come to," said Harold.

"Indeed, I told you he would…eventually," said Teddy.

"Praise be One Paw!" uttered Chipper under his breath.

As you can imagine, I was confused. I had no idea what had happened to me and could only surmise that it must've been serious, for so many of my closest friends and acquaintances were there, looking over me as if I had been terribly ill.

"You've been so sick," said the Mousette who was rubbing my shoulder with her nose. "And you've been unconscious now for four weeks. I called in your friends, most of whom had given up on you already, to witness your awakening."

"This is a significant event in the history of our nation," said Niner. "I have circulated a petition which endorses you, Percy, for President of Sunflower Country. Already it has accumulated five hundred scratches. You will win paws-down should you decide to run."

"Is this true?" I queried, and was stunned by the weak sound of my own voice.

"It is," said Chipper. "You are going to be President of the Greens, Percy. How about that!"

"I am at a loss for words."

"As you should be," said Niner. "What could you have been dreaming, Percy? You were tossing and turning as if a gigantic Snake were after you."

"And you must've sweated off half an ounce in your terrifying display!" said Chipper. "We were all very concerned for your well-being."

"Could I have been poisoned?" I asked, struggling to get to my four feet.

"It is not wholly outside the realm of possibility," said Bobby, "but we tend to think otherwise. You've been under a lot of stress lately. What *were* you dreaming of, Percy? That is all we would like to know."

"I...I...I don't remember," I said, and this was mostly the truth.

"Well, it's good to hear your voice again—that's all I've got to say!" chirped Harold succinctly as he left the room.

Chipper followed him out, saying as he departed, "You've got that right, Harry!"

Bobby and Teddy also filed out, and Teddy remarked on his way, "It's back to politics for you, Percy." He laughed merrily.

Niner gestured with a paw to the two nurses, thanked them for their assistance, and sent them on their way. Now with just Niner and me in the room, I felt much more comfortable being alone with my friend. "What happened to me?" I asked, fully expectant of a disappointing and insufficient response.

"Four weeks ago you came home and fell asleep, or so I am left to presume," Niner mused. "I showed up the next morning, as is my custom; but when I knocked on your door, nobody answered. Naturally, I was concerned. So I did what I hope you would have done had you been in my shoes—I waited. But after a time, I could wait no longer, and I determined to break in. To make a long story short, I found you writhing on your bed like a Snake in heat, most undoubtedly having a violent seizure of some sort. Immediately I called the doctor, who arrived five minutes later to confirm my suspicions—you *were* having a seizure, but he could not tell me why. He just advised you would come out of it soon if I continued to give you water. And that is about all there is to the story, I'm afraid."

"But four weeks! I am incredulous!"

"I know, I know. We were amazed that you lasted so long. At times, you had violent fits, but for a large portion of the time you appeared to be sleeping contentedly. You must be hungry. Here, take a kernel."

Quickly and avidly, I devoured the food Niner offered me, then shook my head. "Get me out of here!" I barked. "And show me this damned petition of yours. I have to see it for myself."

"Certainly. By the way, I got old Tessa to sign it too. That old hag grumbled for hours about it, but finally put her scratch in because she felt sorry for you, being an invalid and whatnot. What do you think of that, Percy? What do you think of that, eh?"

"You're just crazy," I laughed. "Come on, let's get out of here."

My inclination to escape from the stuffiness of my hole needed no reiteration on my part. Niner led me out slowly, for I still felt weak and drunk from my infirmity. To tell the truth, I was beginning to think I had survived Arsenic poisoning by someone who disagreed with my proposals in Congress the day before (or rather, four weeks ago, astonishing as that sounds).

"You are going to like this," said Niner. At the time, I did not know what he was referring to and, speaking frankly, did not care all that much as far as the matter went. After all, I had just awoken from a deep and life-threatening coma. I found out soon enough however, for even before I stepped outside I heard a massive rumbling of Mice beyond my burrow's door.

They were waiting for me—a congregation of over three hundred Mice—the whole wretched lot of them full of squeals and squeaks. "We love Percy! Percy, Percy, Percy! Percy for President!"

I stepped out cautiously, first one foot, then the other, and into a glorious light which bathed my body from head to tail and seemed to purify my very soul. The welcome was stupendous, and after four weeks of being unconscious and of dreaming of Snakes and Men, I can honestly say it was uplifting.

I waved judiciously and tried not to squint my eyes in the glare of the sun. The audience boomed, all together as one, and made such noise as would have raised my father from the dead. A solitary tear hiked its way down my hairy cheek. At last I turned to Niner and spoke, "I have had enough of this. Can we go for a walk to clear my head?"

"Certainly."

Turning back to the crowd one last time, I said, "I thank you all a great deal for coming today; and for all your support and concern, I am graciously in your debt." They seemed to explode in chirps and screams at that moment—ah, and what a moment it was!—before I began to follow Niner on a path behind my burrow that led into the wooded area beyond.

"Come," he said, "your friends are awaiting you. There is much to discuss."

We made our way past massive pine trees, over dormant pine needles, underneath bushes and shrubs and plants of great variety, on a path that led directly into the heart of Fern Valley. The place was famous for Snakes, but intensely beautiful. Ascetics often went there to resolve their tensions and become more at one with nature. It was a place designed specifically by One Paw for the spiritual enjoyment of every Mouse in Sunflower Country.

After several minutes, we rounded a scaly, old tree and began to climb a short hill to our destination. I saw ahead of me all the Senators and Representatives of my country, not to mention the Supreme Justices and, much to my surprise, President Oliver himself. When we finally arrived, every Mouse stood in line to shake my paw. I was flattered beyond humility.

President Oliver grabbed my paw with great force and looked me directly in the eye, saying, "You are destined to be the Mouse on the Mountain, Percy, and one day soon at that. Do you understand the obligations that attend the Presidency?"

"I believe I do."

"Good, that is very good! Remember, it's not okay to tell lies just because they are for your own utility."

"Of course, I agree with you," I said.

"You see! *That* was a lie! You should get comfortable with your own immorality. Better watch what you say, but not too carefully, son."

"I shall keep that in mind."

The President turned abruptly and began talking with one of the Justices, taking up the conversation with so much facility you would have thought they were related. Perhaps they were; after all, in our community many of the Mice were inbred and interrelated in some way, though they were unaware of it. The genetic turmoil that might ordinarily have resulted from excessive inbreeding had fortunately been tempered by the fact that our Government felt a strong duty to allow a large variety of foreign Mice free access to our homeland and its numerous resources. The vast majority of these foreign Mice were completely useless and contributed nothing to society, but our country did not seem to mind this. Once I got in office, I made a personal vow that I would not put a stop to this influx for fear of upsetting that segment of the population, and hence losing their vote.

I sometimes thought that I derived all of my success in politics from an insecurity in making decisions and an unwillingness to resolve any issue assuredly one way or the other. My uncertainty had been met everywhere by smiles and squeals of approval. If I did not come down strong on one side or the other, I could walk the middle line and turn votes my way from both factions. This tactic, heretofore unheard of in Mouse politics, had given me many victories already and would almost surely see me to the Presidency. My perfect, soothing voice and good looks also would have a paw in making me the Mouse on the Mountain.

"Let us get down to business, shall we?" chirped Harold. As if on cue, the other Mice came together in a large circle. There were over twenty of them in all, most of whom leaned forward eagerly to hear what was going to be said next.

"We are convened here today, in a gathering of the most indisputably, incontrovertibly—" began Chipper, before he was rudely interrupted.

"Oh, just get to the point already! Enough with the superfluous babble!" This was a Justice speaking out.

"Very well. I shall comply."

"Then do, by all means."

"We are here to discuss what will happen to our country in the next couple of months. There is an election to be held tomorrow which will decide the Presidency for the upcoming year. It is expected that Percy will be chosen by a landslide and that he will no doubt make an excellent President.

"But there is a new development…" The audience became deathly still for a moment, trying to hear this next tidbit of information. "And I shall now relinquish the discussion to President Oliver to elaborate on the details of this problem."

The Mouse on the Mountain stepped forth and cleared his throat, holding one paw behind his back shrewdly while the other was busy making meaningful gestures in front of him. "Friends, Greens, CountryMice, lend me your little ears. A matter of grave concern now faces our nation. The Blues, as you know, have been building up their military force for some time now and have, in the past year, wholly outstripped us on that front. It is quite possible that now, after many years of peace, the Blues are planning an invasion of Sunflower Country. Add to this the dreadful knowledge that they already have a foot in the door, due to our lenient immigrational policy, and you may easily see what kind of situation we have on our paws. How we shall deal with this problem I am not sure, but that it must be dealt with is beyond all doubt. A spectre is haunting

Sunflower Country—the spectre of Bummunism. As I see it, the years ahead will be most troublesome, most troublesome indeed. Whoever is elected into power will have to contend with this and many other problems. How it will be done I cannot say at the present, but that it will be done, else our nation collapse, is beyond all doubt. I urge you all to think on these matters thoroughly, while you eat and while you sleep even, and to brainstorm several courses of action that we may take should the situation prove as dire as I suspect. Work together, let one Mouse help the other, and most importantly, let us all lend a paw to Percy, who will surely be the next Mouse on the Mountain, to overcome every dilemma he must face with the ease and gracefulness that is granted to us all—all of us Greens—by sacred One Paw above. May heaven bless your souls, each and every one!"

There was a pitter and a patter of applause from a few of the Mice present, but since all of us were so accustomed to speeches of this sort, they did not rile us up much. We looked at it as an opportunity to think things through and to reason out a solution to the problem at paw—the encroachment of Blues in our democracy.

"What we have here," began Harold, "is a situation which could bring demise to our country."

"It is necessary," said Teddy, "that we deal with this as logically and as expeditiously as possible."

"While yet," Bobby intoned, "we must refrain from discriminating against the Blues as Mice, for though they have a different color, that does not make them any less Mice."

"What are we to do?" asked a Representative named Neil.

"I'll tell you," responded Harold. "The only solution to this problem is to put a stop to the immigration. No one ought to be allowed in our boundaries unless he or she is a Green, or a friend or relative of one."

"The bottom line," said Chipper, "is we cannot allow any more Blues into the country without further compromising our national integrity. We simply must put an end to the immigration. What need have we of a bunch of Bums anyhow?"

I spoke out for the first time, "The Bummunists have a philosophy which appeals to the poor and less fortunate of society. To give what belongs inherently to the rich out to all the Bums of the world is patently unfair and will not be allowed to come to pass while I am President of Sunflower Country. When I am securely in office, I shall pass legislation prohibiting the further intrusion of Blues into our society."

"But what if they are disguised as Greens?" asked Neil.

"You can't disguise a Blue, can you?" asked Bobby.

"A Blue is a Blue, a Bummunist is a Bum—there's no disguising that!" declared an outraged Harold.

"We shall have to set up examination points along the border, with specialized police who will be trained to look carefully for disguises," I said calmly.

"Are you making a decision?" asked Harold.

"I must. I am going to be President, aren't I? But the Mice of the world don't have to know about it yet. What is spoken here must remain secret."

"Amazing!"

"Thank you," I responded graciously.

"This meeting is now adjourned!" declared Chipper.

At that, we dispersed. Then Niner led me to his burrow on the third ridge, where I concealed myself until the election results came in. Only one Mouse had the gall to run against me.

I didn't even know his name.

PROMISES

In those glory-filled days prior to my Presidential responsibilities, I was an extremely wealthy Mouse. I brought in over two thousand kernels a month for a grand total of—well, I don't really need to count for you. If my excellent heredity did not prevent it, I could have been a very fat Mouse. It was a great blessing for me to be rich. It allowed me to appear altruistic to my compatriots. I typically gave my excess kernels away to charity and, in so doing, complemented and enhanced my already stupendous reputation. The community saw me as a friendly, caring individual and, to be frank with you, I did not want to disappoint them.

So, though some might think this a self-serving tactic merely to get elected, nothing could have been further from the truth—I gave away fully three thousand kernels that I had in stock to poor and needy Greens the day before the election. It was merely a matter of course. I was going to give them away sooner or later anyhow. What better occasion was there? To boost my standing in the social eye just prior to the casting of votes could not have been more availing to my track record. I was a nice guy—there was no getting around it—and the Mice of my country were well aware of it.

The word got out about my immense generosity, but that alone would not prove sufficient to win the race. I had to give a speech—the most grand and fabulous speech of my entire life—if I was to have a hope of succeeding in this important adventure. I prepared for three complete hours, memorized all my lines, mastered all my nervous tics, and rehearsed all my facial movements and paw gestures to the point of perfection. If there could be found any flaw in the speech as I had prepared it, I would have gladly tossed out another three thousand kernels to the lucky critic who spotted it.

Thus it happened one fine day that I found waiting for me on the other side of a mushroom podium what seemed a thousand Mice, perhaps even more. There was a great deal of applause at first, but as I became more comfortable in front of this massive gathering of Mice, the noise began to diminish, slowly at first, then suddenly, until all was quiet. At that precise moment, I began to speak.

"Good citizens of Sunflower Country, there stands before me today a myriad collection of the most intelligent and prudent Mice in all the world, a group that will decide today at the polls, with one scratch for each individual, the very fate of our nation in the next year. For it is this group, this myriad collection of Mice, which will determine who becomes President for an entire year of our existence, and which, moreover, will select by a longstanding Constitutional right the Mouse who will lead this country, Sunflower Country, a country that faces many new and many existing challenges, into an enigmatic and at best uncertain future, where the possibility of increased Snake attacks, the nightmare of Human intervention for humanitarian and utilitarian purposes, at the expense of all good Mice, treads heavily upon all of our hearts, as we approach an era in which it will be necessary to expand far beyond our borders and journey to and colonize new, strange, and distant lands, in addition to prohibiting unwanted immigration into our borders by the dreaded Blues, a group of Bummunist extremists who will most certainly bring our beautiful land to outright ruin and collapse if we happen to permit them such liberty.

"I first and foremost want to assure you that, although Snake attacks have become increasingly frequent over the past year, they will not become more prevalent under my tenure. Should I be elected President, I shall augment our Army with a Watch Patrol that is specifically designed to look out for the abominable presence of slimy Snakes in our country, and to give the warning so that all Mice can seek retreat from the danger at paw. Indeed, this obligation is at the forefront of my list of things to accomplish. And you are probably wondering at this point, 'What haven may we run to in our critical time of need? Where can we run in order to escape the vicious fork-tongued fiend?' The answer to these questions, I assure you, good Mice, is far from simple, but already I have employed our most ingenious engineers to deal with the problem and have proposed a challenge to them to design and complete the project as soon as possible. In my first couple of weeks in office, I promise that we shall construct a device that will ward off every Snake from every burrow in Sunflower Country. The problem of Snakes will be no more, the threat of the fork-tongued fiend will be gone from our peaceful lives forever, when I am elected.

"Human intervention in our lives has in the past been a serious dilemma for our kind. I seek to redress the wrongs done by the great two-footed, two-handed beast. As with the Snakes, a warning system will be established so that, when the white-coated Men appear to sneak us off to their scientific laboratories and perform One Paw-only-knows what sort of experiments upon us, we shall do what heretofore we have never considered doing in the face of such peril—we shall high-tail it into the woods and run for our lives. Those unable to do this will have to stay behind and feign death and hope that they will be ignored, but the healthy among us will have ample opportunity to escape. This is the most logical and expeditious manner in which we can survive as a family, as a clan, and as a united body of Greens in Sunflower Country.

"We are now reaching an era in which it will become necessary to colonize new lands, explore uncharted territories, and expand far beyond our borders. Our relations with the other Mice of this world can only be described as coarse and unfriendly. When I am elected to office, I shall see to it that our relations are positive and benevolent, and that the economy of Sunflower Country benefits from such sapient and fruitful alliances. Immediately upon entering my Presidential office, I shall order expedition teams to be sent out into the distant countryside for the express purpose of discovering what lies beyond the Two Rivers, into lands that we have not yet explored adequately, and for the purpose of probing suitable places for our Mice to settle. The last census, tallied while I was unconscious in bed, indicates that our numbers now exceed three thousand. Just half a year ago they were less than one thousand. We are growing exponentially, while yet the land upon which we live remains the same size. I have a solution to this problem, if only the world will listen, if only the world will elect me President of Sunflower Country.

"Recently, I have been informed that our country is being invaded by unwanted immigrants. Folks, this is the most serious problem of them all, for these immigrants I have been further informed are *Blues!* If we allow our country to be infiltrated with more immigrants, our population will grow that much faster, while if we stand by and let in our gates those whom we know to be Blues and Bummunists to the core, we are not only compromising our very nationalistic integrity, we are conceding our souls in the struggle for existence. May we send the dreaded Blues back to their dreadful homeland, may we banish all wretched Bummunists from our free and anti-Bummunist nation for once and for all! Let us put a stop to unwanted immigration! Give me your vote, I implore you, and you will see it come to an end!

"I am your last and only hope at saving Sunflower Country and preserving the sacred lives within it. I am your last and only hope at saving you from Snake attacks, from Human intervention, and from the unwanted immigration of Blues into our blessed country. I am the oldest and wisest of all the Mice in Congress. I have been an Historian for ten long years; therefore, I alone know the demands of a good Government. Use your common sense this afternoon, good Mice, and vote with good judgment and intelligence. Vote Percy for President! Thank you, and One Paw bless Sunflower Country!"

When my speech ceased, the assembled Mice broke into a clamor and an applause that continued for several minutes. It was clear that anyone running against me would not stand a chance. At that moment, I had won the Presidency paws-down.

I ambled out amidst the crowd and began the laborious process of shaking paws and kissing infants. I was honestly grateful for all the support and found myself flushing on more than one occasion when, for example, someone would say, "You're the best, Percy!" or "We love you, Percy!" or even "You'll make the greatest President in Sunflower Country history!" These and many more exclamations of veneration met my ears and pleased me immensely. I must be honest, never before in my life had I felt so vibrant and full of health, so confident and brilliant, as I did then, walking among all the beautiful Mice of my country. Never before had I felt so sure of something that was not yet defined.

When all this was done, I was escorted out of the field by the resident Secret Service members, a clan of some twenty Mice whose only duty it was to protect a Mouse in power, and I was taken to Niner's headquarters to await the election results, which would come in later that evening, when all the scratches had been counted.

Once there, Niner accosted me, "You make a lot of promises. You intend to keep all those promises?"

"I am a politician, Niner," I began patiently. "Don't get me wrong. I mean well enough, but words are just words—we use them for the utilitarian purpose of advancing our power and happiness. It is as I suspected—the Mice of our country are extremely gullible. Like men, they believe in what they want to be true, nothing more and nothing less. If I had said I was going to cut the kernel tax rate by fifty percent, I would have had them drooling on me. The truth of the matter is I'm not going to do anything about unwelcome foreigners because, after all, they now constitute a large segment of the population. I shall need their votes when I go up for re-election next year."

Niner considered these words carefully before responding, "So what about the Snake problem? Are you going to do anything about that?"

"I shall support the futile tinkering with contraptions, and I suppose I shall set up a Watch Patrol as I have promised."

"Is that a promise?"

"It is."

"Good. You know, I lost a relative to a Snake two years ago, a cousin named Tardy. When he was late once again for a family get-together, nobody paid any notice; but three days later when he still didn't turn up we were left to presume that a Snake had had him for dinner. It was later confirmed that the tracks went straight through his burrow."

"Niner, I want you to know that, as a friend you can trust, I shall do my best to maintain the safety of the Mice in my country. Over my dead body will Snakes have their way here. You understand?"

"Thanks, Percy. You know, you're a great pal. If for some reason—"

"Look, there's Harold!" I shouted gleefully.

Sure enough, Harold had come down Niner's burrow bearing good news, no doubt. The fat Mouse scurried into the room, his tail stretching far behind him, and bowed low to the ground.

"I come with good news, Master Percy: the early polling surveys, with approximately thirty percent reporting, indicate that you are ahead by a wide margin. You now lead by ninety-five percent. How's that for good news!"

"Wonderful!" I exclaimed. I was nearly too embarrassed to ask who my opposition was, but at last marshaled the resolve. "Who am I running against, Harold? Do you have a clue?"

"Some short-tailed shrift named Zander," Harold answered, "who has obvious Bummunist views on certain issues."

"No wonder he's trailing so badly," I blurted.

"Well, if you think about it, five percent for a Bummunist is not bad in an anti-Bummunist country like ours."

"Who do you think would vote for him?"

"Bums, by and large."

"It figures," I conceded. "The fact that he has a short tail would also contribute heavily to his loss."

"That is true," said Harold. "No Female is going to vote for a Mouse with a short tail. Appearance has much to do with whether or not one will get elected."

"Well, thank you, Harold, for your benevolent tidings. I shall keep you and the rest of my friends close to heart in this critical time."

"Good luck, Percy, though doubtless you will not need it." With that, Harold turned tail and scampered out of the hole.

When he was gone, Niner treated me to a sunflower kernel and a mug of Alertness Elixer, which were more than welcome. The silence of Niner's burrow became unbearable after just a few minutes. I turned to my friend and asked, "What do you think will be the deciding factor in my getting elected?"

Niner reflected for a moment, scratched his chin with a scruffy claw, then gave an honest and unbiased response, which was more than I could ask coming from a close friend: "You know, Percy, you are a good-looking Mouse in your old age—few could deny your handsome features, and your extraordinary virility will certainly not go unnoticed by all the Female Mice of our country. But that is not the only reason, not by a long shot. You are also a wonderful and eloquent speaker, capable of charming thousands by batting your eyelashes and manipulating the accent of your voice. In addition, you have fairly good ideas about Government and, lest we forget, have a reputation for dependability, a reputation for steadfastness in times of confusion, and, finally, a reputation for generosity to those around you. Though only an average Mouse in other respects, it cannot be denied that you are the perfect politician."

"Thank you, Niner. You're a true pal. That's just what I wanted to hear."

On through the night the weather turned cold. My ascendancy was to be bittersweet, for this nobody named Zander, the one with the short tail, ended up garnering twenty percent of the vote, which was proof enough that a good portion of the population was discontented about one thing or another.

Perhaps now is as good a time as any to elaborate on the theory and practice of Bummunism. The theory is rather simple: it is based on the premise that a Mouse should not have to work for anything in life, that everything ought to be handed to him on a golden platter; it does away with all competition and ensures that everyone will have an equal share of success; it promotes obesity and laziness, being supported primarily by the despondent members of society. It hails all the Bums in Mousedom and advocates that they unite under a common banner—the exalted banner of indolence.

The theory is grossly altered in practice. Poor, helpless Mice mooch off the rich and conscientious, thus bringing the economy to a grinding halt. The country collapses on the momentum of its own ineptness. Everyone who stays in the country eventually becomes a Bum and feeds off the hardworking Mice of the land. Eventually, the rich defect and go somewhere else, leaving the Bums to disintegrate in their wake. And, as a country's success is dictated by the success of its economy, so the country falls apart completely and utterly when left to such a demise. The Bums regroup and travel to different places, thereby ensuring that the process will recur in the future.

It was my opinion, and the opinion of nearly all wealthy Mice, that Bummunism was a jeopardy to Government and a disease to all nations. It just seemed wrong for the lazy Bums of the world to get their way and leech off the industrious members of society. Why did I have to pay for someone else to breathe? Every Mouse ought to breathe his own air.

My country was founded on freedom. As President-Elect, I had promised that it would stay that way for as long as I was in office. I had also promised that Bummunism would be stopped in this glorious land I called home and that I would do everything in my power to eradicate this unwelcome parasite. To succeed, I merely had to compromise the power of the vote and my potential for re-election.

But what is a promise?

THE PROPHET'S WARNING

The year started out strongly for me, then steadied into a boring tedium, punctuated by moments of excitement, before finally twisting itself into a smashing and extraordinary conclusion. I went about my job as rigorously and as diligently as possible, making various appearances as I saw fit.

I was deemed a good President, though certainly not a great one.

Snake attacks steadily worsened, as we lost fourteen Mice to the fork-tongued heathen over the course of the year. My plans to warn everyone of their coming were thwarted by how scentless and soundless these predators can be. Indeed, many of my guards were the first victims. I wholeheartedly supported the research necessary to prevent additional bloodshed.

As I had promised Niner, I did next to nothing about illegal aliens and unwanted immigration of Blues into the country. This passivity concerning Bummunism earned me a few enemies, not to mention a few friends. The Bums were clearly encroaching, but there was little threat of them taking over the country, and so I was forced to conclude that my friends were just anxious to foment some kind of purging of all the Blues. I calculated that my total vote could increase by ten percent if all the Blues cast their scratches for me in the next election.

And to tell the truth, I was having a great time as President; I actively sought re-election. Another term for me, another name in the history books—that's how I thought of it. During my term, I was almost certain that re-election would be inevitable, especially since I was still a hero in the eyes of the majority of the public. I even had the gall to figure I could garner ninety percent of the vote next time around, for though I had accomplished little to ward off the Snakes and the white-coated Men, though I had not brought a halt to the influx of unwelcome foreigners, though in most respects I was an average President (largely because of the fact that I had not been given ample opportunity to prove my worth), I sensed that the country was pleased with its progress, pleased with the efforts at expansion, however foundering and ultimately disappointing they were, pleased in a general sense with me and my leadership.

I had my corps of supporters who would stick by me through thick and thin, who would always be there to shake my frail paw and shower me with compliments, such as, "Percy, you're doing a wonderful job. Sunflower Country is blessed to have you as its President."

Foreign affairs were prevailing against the odds. I had called a truce with the Blues at last and organized a peace process around which the separate nations could prosper. Economically, we were thriving. The market was more than just riding on the wave of Oliver's presidency. We were setting records and making progress every day and in every way imaginable.

One day, about half-way through my term, while I was skipping along and minding my own business, with several guards nearby attending to me and trying desperately to keep up with me—I prided myself in being in excellent shape for a twelve-year-old—a strange and frightening thing happened to me.

Out from behind a burrow limped a Mouse far older than even I myself. He intercepted me in my morning jog, for which I had become quite well-known in the neighborhood. He was leaning on an old, gnarled twig, every hair on his body having turned an undignified and feeble gray. Knowing full well the identity of the Mouse, I made an inconspicuous attempt to skirt around this obstruction.

"Where are you going?" he asked in a raspy voice that betrayed excessive maturity. I replied nothing, but continued along on my way as if I had not heard him.

His next words, however, grasped my attention and held it fast: "You're going to die, Percy!" I stopped in my tracks and, turning on my heels, accosted the elderly wretch, a poor old Mouse named Bleet, commonly known as the prophet of Sunflower Country.

"As you may know, old Bleet," I gravely announced, "I am not one who depends upon the voice of prophets to dictate my every course of action. Not a Mouse am I who will stand idly by while the impotent words of false magicians and toothless soothsayers sway the public's general opinion. I care not for doomsday logic and palm-reading antics from you and your kind. Begone with all your vain prophecy and ridiculous sophistries! As President of Sunflower Country I can have your neck if you so much as speak another word to me. Hear?"

"I hear fine in my old age, young Percy," he said, unperturbed, "though perhaps you yourself ought to tune your ears to another frequency—perhaps that would be the wise and judicious thing to do—whilst I relate to you a bit of dreadful knowledge that, due to the wisdom of many, many years, has been rendered comprehensible to me alone."

"You speak like a true MadMouse," I began, though now interested in what more old Bleet had to say. "Continue," I gestured with my paw.

"The death of all Greens hangs above us like a menacing cloud in the sky," he said. "Our future is damned, to be sure. The Blues are coming! The Blues are coming! And because you have done nothing to stifle the flow of unwanted immigrants into this beloved country, you will live to see the day when this beloved country falls from its seemingly invincible perch as One Paw's most sacred land and gathering of Mice into the dark desperation that we all know accompanies every Bummunist movement. If the world were meant to be a host to the parasites who are now taking over this land, then so let it be; but on the other hand, if you had had any conscience left at all in that politically-persuaded mind of yours, you would have taken action long ago to drive all Bums and Blues from our borders. But alas, it is too late for that! Your only hope now is that you refrain from selling any secrets to the Bummunists and that, at all costs, you maintain an aura of respectability and morality in the eyes of your compatriots. This I have spoken and shall speak no more. Goodbye to you, Percy, and good luck!"

Bleet staggered his way into his burrow, limping terribly on his left foot, which had suffered an old battle wound from times preceding my birth. I watched helplessly as he went, wishing that I could continue the conversation, but prophets such as Bleet were all the same, always short-winded and seeking, more often than not, merely to upset you with their dire prognostications.

'Bah!' I thought, as I dismissed the aged fool from my mind. When was the last time any prophet discovered the truth about anything? Never in my lifetime. Besides, as a Mouse in power, I could readily afford to dismiss all threats and would-be mystical assumptions. The Blues had never been a real danger, and Bummunism itself, as a philosophy and way of life, had always found itself the object of needless prejudice at the paws of unthinking Westerners such as Bleet himself.

No, I thought, I would simply try to befriend myself with every Bum in Sunflower Country, thereby stealing votes from Zander when I went up for re-election at the end of the year. In my prolonged experience as a politician I had learned one thing very well—nothing mattered besides the vote. The number of votes I garnered would determine the power at my very clawtips. What I could do with that power—aha, there was the rub!—was determined by the factions to which I was beholden (and that included but a meager portion of the citizens who had voted for me). All of Government is mere puppetry—I was under hidden strings of influence and the Mice of this country were being controlled by me. Sometimes when I thought about it, I just wanted to laugh.

Even still, the words of Bleet had struck something of a chord in me; I fancied that if I had actually made a mistake, it would reflect poorly on my ability to lead the country, and I would not be reelected, much less scratched about favorably in the history books.

Narcissism—what is it? Is it, as most Mice are wont to think, fascination with self-image? I think not. In fact, the more I think about it, narcissism is more fascination with substance, the substance of self. That made me, Percy, more or less the most narcissistic Mouse in the entire world. But for some reason or other, this did not concern me as much as perhaps it should have. I realized that I was a bit arrogant, a shade overconfident, somewhat deceitful, and, all in all, lacking in moral restraint, but did that make me any less a good President? Less a Mouse, perhaps, but—*less a President?*

These thoughts ran through my mind as I was sitting in my office, in a pile of cedar shavings in the corner, and in general passing my Government time doing nothing as usual while I eagerly awaited my next opportunity at a public exhibition. Getting paid by the Government meant no more, no less.

At length my thoughts were interrupted when I heard a scratch at my door, which was simply an oversized cedar chip, easily shoved aside for entry. "Come in!" I announced impatiently.

The next thing I knew, old Tessa, the prostitute from my neighborhood who had put her scratch in my favor while I was unconscious, stepped cautiously into my office and bowed low to the ground. I had expected her earlier, but was not at all displeased by her tardiness.

"Good afternoon, President Percy." Her voice sounded strained, as if she had been crying recently. I asked her what was wrong, but she concealed her emotions expertly, revealing nothing of her inner state of mind.

Later, after we had had our share of pleasures, I repeated my question, curiosity waxing: "What is the matter with you today, Tessa? Don't you enjoy me anymore? Am I not good enough for you?"

"No, no. It's nothing like that," she said, before continuing hesitantly, "it's just that…I know you've been sleeping with other Mice and…and it's not a great comfort to know that I am sharing cedar shavings with other whores. You do understand me, don't you? As President, you really ought to be married. Promiscuity does not become you. If word gets out that you're sleeping around, it could wreak havoc on your currently impeccable reputation."

"What do you mean?" I replied angrily. "I thought it was common knowledge that Presidents used their authority to take advantage of Female Mice, used their clout to get whatever they damned well wanted."

"Still, you know it's not right."

"Are you telling me you don't like me, Tessa? Is that what I detect, that loathing in your voice? Or are you just burning with jealousy over my other seventeen mistresses?"

"Dear One Paw! I did not know it was that many!"

"Get out!" I heard myself scream. "I hate you and all the rest of them. Good for only one thing—instant pleasure! No brain at all! Is it any wonder that your kind weren't meant to be politicians? You can't be lazy and fat with grace!"

"But, Mr. President?"

"Out!"

The cedar chip slammed as she made herself scarce.

I thought to myself how silly it was that usually I received the majority of my advice from Senators and Representatives, Mice of Government such as myself, while in the past few days a prophet and a whore had taken their turns at reproaching me. As a politician, my shortcomings were few, but Tessa had pointed out a weakness I had as a Mouse, and Bleet had attacked me from another front—that of negligence on my part as commander of Sunflower Country. Perhaps both of them were right. Perhaps my philandering, a self-indulgent pastime for me that in no way hindered my ascent to the Presidency, would become public knowledge and the media would have their way with me, tearing me to shreds with their words and breaching the security of my moral constitution. So what if I thought that I was right? In their eyes I would be wrong and I would be subsequently forced into martyrdom, compromising my ability to get reelected. It required a somewhat greater leap of faith to believe that Blues were infiltrating our country, threatening to assume power and drive out all Greens. But I entertained that thought as well, considering the possible ramifications should this unlikely scenario come to pass.

As a politician, I was malleable. I could bend this way and that to please my subjects. I could say one thing and mean another without the risk of conceding my character. What matter whether I were leading a country full of Greens or Blues? All I cared for was that I was leading the country. All other considerations could fall by the wayside. At any rate, I figured my leniency towards the Blues would reap enough votes to more than compensate for the losses I would suffer should my numerous love escapades be disclosed.

There came another rapping at my door.

"Come in," I said.

Harold peeped his head through the opening and said tentatively, "Percy?"

"Yes, Harold?"

"May I have a moment of your time, most gracious sir? There is something we need to discuss."

"Certainly. Come in."

The Mouse seemed reluctant, as if uncertain whether or not he were intruding upon my precious spare time.

"Percy," he said, "I couldn't help but overhear what old Tessa said to you. It seems that she has a good point after all, and I, along with numerous other important Mice would like to encourage you to take a stand on this issue, and to make a final decision as to whom you may be willing to spend the rest of your life with. We would all like to see you happily married."

"So, you were eavesdropping?"

"Your voices were so obstreperous, the encounter hardly evinced itself as clandestine."

"Stop talking like that," I said.

"Like what, Percy?"

"Like some erudite literary professor. I hate that."

"But sir, you must realize that Tessa was right. If word got out about your numerous mistresses, you would be up the creek without a paddle."

"Stop doing that," I said.

"Doing what, Percy?"

"Using stupid clichés with me. You do realize I am a well-educated Mouse, don't you?"

"Of course. I had no intention of offending you. It seems like just yesterday we were best friends, bantering with each other in Congress. But you've certainly changed since then, haven't you? You won't take a word of advice from even your oldest buddy anymore."

"No offense taken. And you are still my best friend, Harold. I've just been a little on edge lately. Perhaps I need some time off. A vacation? Yes, that will do."

"But, sir?"

"I know what you're thinking, Harold, and you are probably right—I need a wife to stand by my side and lead me to great and exotic pleasures in the bedroom. I should do away with all my mistresses—I did not want to tell Tessa, but there are really more than eighteen of them you know—and settle down. It will suit me well in the critical eye of the public…"

"Then who will it be?"

"Who will be what?" I asked, mindlessly.

"Who will be your wife?"

"Oh I suppose Tessa is as good as any. She's not the best looking but she has such regal poise, and does not crumble under pressure— qualities to be desired in any First Mousette. Schedule the wedding for tomorrow afternoon."

"Yes sir," said Harold, who betrayed the faintest hint of a smile as he left the room.

A WEDDING

The circumstances of my marriage to Tessa would not otherwise have been important were it not for the fact that I almost lost my life in the process. For that reason alone I think it necessary to divulge the details of that strangest of days in the summer of my first term as President of Sunflower Country.

On the day of my wedding the heat was oppressive and clung to my fur coat like used bubble gum. I found myself feeling faint on a number of occasions throughout the ceremony, though Tessa herself revealed no distress. She just cast her emotional glances my way, tears welling up in her feminine eyes, while I made the vain attempt to appear conciliatory, smiling insincerely back at her. I was not at all perturbed by this charade.

"Do you," droned the priest, who appeared ill on account of the heat, "Percy, take Tessa to be your lawfully wedded wife…" As his voice faded into a melancholy hum, my mind drifted to unpleasant thoughts. I thought that as I made this enormous decision, this decision that amounted to self-incarceration and prolonged sexual inhibition, I was following in the footsteps of my father, a Mouse whom I had come to hate in the latter years of his life. He had lived his entire life in vain, a vehement anti-Bummunist who never wasted a word without condemning "those damned Blues." His final injunction to me, while he was lying upon his cedar-chip deathbed, had been simply this: "See to it, son, that you vanquish all Bummunists from this wonderful land!" I had shaken my head no, but not before he had closed his eyes and consumed his last breath of air.

"Well?" asked the priest.

"Well what?" I returned.

"Do you, or don't you?" He must have seen the look of perplexity in my expression, for, barely a moment later, the priest continued sarcastically, "Take Tessa to be your lawfully wedded wife, to have and to hold, blah-blah-blah, so long as you both shall live?"

"I suppose."

"That's more like it." Then, turning to Tessa, he said, "And do you Tessa, take Percy…"

Again, I lost interest in the discourse. My thoughts strayed to Bummunism. I did not, for one, see my father's dreaded nemesis as anything of a threat. After all, we were living in a land that was quite literally defined by the power of Infinite Expansionalism, which basically granted us the right to grow and prosper endlessly at the expense of our smaller neighbors. So what if a few Blues made it inside our borders? As a politician, I realized that the smart thing to do was to befriend them and ensure that their votes were scratched in my favor in the next election. I saw no threat of the Blues invading and taking over my beautiful country.

"What One Paw hath joined, let not Mouse put asunder!" The applause roused me from my reverie. "You may kiss the bride."

I leaned forward slowly—one might say, *romantically*—and pecked Tessa on her hairy cheek. It hardly amounted to a true kiss, but I had a reputation to maintain, after all, and did not want to appear overly risqué.

The reception was magnificent by anyone's standards. All of my friends were there to accompany me, a band of loyal sycophants beginning with Niner and ending with Neil, each of whom had his rehearsed set of compliments ready when I approached. The food was delectable, a veritable banquet that stretched as far as the eye could see in either direction, of rice and corn and bread and fruit and—dear One Paw, *cheese!* Somebody had even discovered and brought along a box of Man cereal, and upon each palatable flake one could put a mouth-watering quantity of peanut butter.

I busied myself at this great feast with personally thanking everyone who had come. It was a crucial task to first shake with my right paw, grasp the elbow sturdily with my left, nod and pretend to pay especially close attention, then peck all the wives' cheeks very discreetly, and nod and pretend some more. I concealed the intense boredom that I felt at this event with a grace and an ease that could only be described as extremely professional.

At last it was back to discussing politics and, as usual, the topic of conversation eventually drifted towards the Bummunists.

"They are staging a rebellion, you know?" said Teddy, a piece of cheese hanging uncouthly from his whiskers.

"Certainly you don't mean the Blues, do you?" asked Harold.

"No, I mean the Bummunists."

"What difference is there between a Blue and a Bummunist?" I could not refrain myself from asking.

"A Bummunist does not necessarily have to be a Blue, but a Blue must, of necessity, be a Bum. That is the logic of it, or so I'm told."

"Funny logic, to be sure," growled Chipper.

"Of what rebellion do you speak, good Teddy?" I queried.

"The violent uprising that is to occur during the ides of October, consisting of no less than four hundred angry Bummunists, under the auspices and leadership of the excessively cruel and ever-scheming Mouse named Zander."

"Dear One Paw," exclaimed Harold, "what shall we do?" He turned to me expectantly, assuming that I had an answer to this problem, but in all honesty, I was just as confounded as he. What in One Paw's name could the damned Bummunists be up in arms about? Hadn't I fed them well, taken care of all their needs, seen to it that they were given fair representation and the capacity to vote?

I turned from my comrades and feigned contemplation, wrinkling my brow judiciously. "If we are going to solve this problem," I began ponderously, "we must know the cause of it. Does anyone here know why our fellow Bummunist citizens are so upset?" For the longest and most uncomfortable span of time, nobody answered.

Then emitted a reply from across the way, from a hoarse voice that seemed to betray a good deal of deep bitterness and lasting resentment. "I'll tell you why they're angry."

The crowd parted to let through a Mouse of small proportions whose tail dangled embarrassingly short behind him, though he was otherwise fair-looking. What happened next cannot be easily described; for, you see, all of time seemed to collapse as one event followed the next in a series that occurred at hyper-blinding speed. At first, I saw the Mouse move as if in a shimmering dream towards me, the distance between seeming exponentially vast, like there was no way he could ever make it to me. Then I saw the flash of silver in his paw—a human tack and a vicious weapon—and stood by helplessly, in the very same trance that had consumed my friends, as this heathen approached so swiftly he appeared to be flying along on winged heels.

Before I realized what was happening, there was an instrument of death at my throat and the Mouse who had taken me hostage was screaming orders to everyone around us.

"Back off! Back off or he dies! I swear to One Eye I shall do it! Go away, clear a path, make way for the future leader of your country!" The crowd parted like sliced cheese and I was rudely jerked forth to an unknown destination.

"It's that short-tailed Bummunist, Zander!" I heard someone exclaim.

I was treated roughly by my adversary, who apparently retained hard feelings towards me, lingering hatred no doubt from the devastating loss he had suffered at my paws in the previous election. He swung my body left and right to ward off any would-be heroes and, on more than one occasion, tripped over my feet which were trailing lifelessly underneath him, my body sagging and lacking energy. The entire experience resembled one of my dreaded nightmares. I looked into the eyes of my friends and family and saw in them a helplessness so utterly absolute it made me want to cry. But I could not blame them, after all. I certainly wouldn't have risked saving their necks had our situations been reversed. We politicians are quite the cowards that we appear.

The vicious criminal, while beating me in the head at frequent intervals with his left paw, kept the tack focused on my neck with his right, and pressed the weapon hard enough to produce a spot of blood. When we had struggled and made our perilous, clumsy way up a nearby hill, he turned to the gathering of Mice in our wake and addressed them formally, in that same hoarse voice which he had used earlier: "My name is Zander. I am the leader of the Bummunist party. If ever you wish to see your President alive again, you will follow my every instruction. For now, be satisfied with the knowledge that he is in my custody, and will remain as such until I see fit to release him.

The only alternative to strict obedience is Percy's untimely departure. His fate rests not in my paws, but in yours. I look forward to doing business with you."

As we departed, the crowd disappeared on the other side of the hill. I unwittingly was the source of as much grief for Zander, in his kidnapping, as he was for me, and for the same reason; for without having to try, I was making the entire project incredibly difficult for him.

"Where are you taking me?" I asked the Mouse whom I had to assume now was a dangerous enemy. Kudos to me—I revealed not a trace of fear in my voice.

He did not answer me immediately, but, rather, grunted with the exertion of having to practically lug my body forth. At length, between gulps of air, the Mouse loosened his grip and, keeping the weapon firm against my jugular, spoke: "You will find out soon enough."

"That's not exactly reassuring," I ventured. "Do you truly mean to take my life?"

"Only if they don't do as I say."

"What in the name of One Paw do you want?"

"It's very simple," he said gruffly, "I want what's best for society— fair and equal treatment of the quiescent class."

"Bums?"

"Some have called us that. But I prefer to think of us as *operationally disadvantaged*."

"A euphemism?"

"Some call it that. But I prefer to call it an *expressional masquerade*."

"But haven't I done enough for you Bums already? Are you not content with your newfound liberties? What more could you possibly ask for? Be specific. Name it, and I shall personally see to it that you have it."

"All of that will be explained in due course. For now, shut up and stop dragging your feet!"

I did my best to comply, considering the fact that my life was at stake, and concentrated on alternating steps with my feet, a task which occupied my complete attention. Neither Zander nor I spoke for the longest time. The silence was eerie and overwhelming.

I noticed that we were making our way to familiar territory—the southern edge of Fern Valley and a wooded area where I had spent the great majority of my childhood playing games. As my captor's grip on the tack gradually relaxed, I paid closer heed to my surroundings. Everywhere we went there was the shade that was so liberally provided by the proliferation of green ferns and other shrubs and plants. The forest floor was covered in brown pine needles. Birds were singing in the far reaches of the canopy, way above us. I thought to myself, 'What a beautiful place!' and under ordinary circumstances wouldn't it have been even more beautiful? But always on the edge of my awareness lurked the dangerous Snakes that inhabited this area. Around every corner I fancied we would meet the fangs of a giant Copperhead or a Coral Snake. I prayed vigilantly for my safety in this exploit.

Zander seemed untroubled by the threat of Snakes, Men, or anything else for that matter, as we plowed our way through this life-abundant jungle.

Suddenly I noticed directly ahead of us a veritable wall of shrubbery. "There's no way through that!" I exclaimed.

"Nonsense! Watch and see!"

Without further ado, he dragged me limb-by-limb into this monstrosity. For the most frightening of moments, we were surrounded by an impenetrable darkness. All the leaves and foliage with which we made contact seemed wet with dew, even at midday. I realized then that the sun never made it down to this layer of the forest floor.

Then at last, when I could take it no more and was about to scream, we made it through…only to find ourselves trapped inside a metal Man-made cage. I turned on my heels and began clawing back the way we had come, but alas, it was too late. The hinges to the door creaked loudly and the gate came swinging down, ensnaring us in this horrifying metal contraption with no hope of escape.

I wheeled angrily on Zander, for he had let go of me inside the cage: "Look what you have done! We are going to die now, you fool! All hope is lost! Don't you know, Man is our greatest enemy!"

Surprisingly, Zander maintained his calm and composure beneath this barrage of chastisement. "We shall get out of this soon enough," he said. "I have friends nearby who will help us." And with that, he began to hoot and holler like a MadMouse for his friends to come and save us.

It seemed decades before help finally arrived. First we heard movement in the foliage, then we saw a nose peek through the bushes, followed shortly thereafter by a pair of eyes, a head and, at last, a body and a tail.

"Thank One Paw you are here, Darian," said Zander. "I don't know what would have happened to us if you hadn't shown up."

But Darian was not interested in helping us get out, and who could blame him, he was interested only in saving his own hide. "There's Snakes around here! Run for your lives!" Consequently, he started scurrying off in the direction he had come, without awaiting further instruction on our part.

Zander called him back, however, and Darian reluctantly turned and slowly began ambling back towards us. When he reached the cage he said only this: "You will be safe, so long as you are in this cage, Master, but fear not—we shall come and get you out again when the threat of Snakes is gone."

He peered at us through the wires of the enclosure for a brief moment of time and hesitated, the very definition of fear emphasizing the look in his eyes. That one moment of hesitation would cost him his life.

With a sickening blow, the Snake's massive jaws snapped around Darian's body and the fangs locked into the sides of the poor Mouse. Darian screamed, but it was a cry of futility at that point. We watched in horror and perverse fascination from behind the safety of the wire as this poor Mouse first squealed in agony, then fell silent as the blood coursed down his fur coat and he was dragged away.

CAPTURED

With Darian's upper body totally engulfed in its mouth and his back legs cycling weakly in the air, the Snake turned its head toward us, its evil eyes bearing the threat of an ultimate return for us. Terror is lent its very definition from moments such as that. I was so frightened my bladder spilled over and the stench of urine became pervasive. If Zander was afraid, it did not show in his countenance; he simply pinched his nose with his paw and cursed me for a coward in a consequently high-pitched, nasal squeal.

But time has a funny way of numbing your fear, and as we waited and waited for someone to come, whether Man or Mouse, all thoughts of danger dissipated. We decided that since there was nothing better to do, we would sit down one end of the cage and discuss, among other things, One Paw and politics.

"So whom do you believe in," asked Zander, "One Eye or One Paw?"

"I don't really care, but One Paw is the one I usually pray to."

"Is that all that the sacred One Paw means to you?"

"I'm sorry, should He have meant more?"

"You are so shallow, Percy. I cannot comprehend why the Mice of Sunflower Country saw you fit to lead them."

"Let's just say I'm a better Mouse than you. Also I am better looking to the Mousettes because of a longer tail."

"Damn this tail!" shouted Zander, suddenly furious. "You know I don't deserve it. It was passed down to me by my father. I was genetically predisposed."

"I'm sorry to say, your predisposition is one of failure. One Paw has damned you and your kind. The Bummunists are condemned here."

"Is that what you think?

"It is."

"You are blind to your own prejudices, Percy. Don't you see, that's just what they want you to think? Open your mind, for once, and view the world from my perspective. That I am a Blue, or you are a Green, does not make either one of us any less of a Mouse. You may yet find that the opinions of the Bummunists agree with your fancy."

"Oh sure. Now you're going to tell me you believe in One Eye."

"I *do* believe in One Eye, but that's not the question. All Blues believe in One Eye. The question is, are you going to cast judgment upon me because of my beliefs? Because of my coat color? Because I am a Bum?"

The conversation was starting to make me uncomfortable. I did not want Zander, nor any Mouse for that matter, turning the tables on me and pointing out how hollow my prejudices were, how vacant at the very foundation were all of my most cherished conceits. I had been brought up to believe that Bummunism was inherently evil. Now to discover that it was just another way of thinking about the world—well, to put it lightly, the revelation was upsetting.

"Who are you," I began, somewhat flustered, "to say that I can or cannot cast judgment upon the Bummunists and their opposing points of view?"

"And who are you," he countered angrily, "to cast judgment? One Eye? One Paw?"

"I have lived my entire life without concern for you and your thoughts, Zander. I can live the remainder in peace as well, so long as you stop pestering me about it. Beliefs are beliefs. You have yours. I have mine. What difference does it make, in the end, whether the country is ruled by Blues or Greens? All that matters to me is that I am the ruler, and as ruler, I determine your place in my country. Your place, and the place of all Bums, is on the southern edge, in the middle of the Drylands, with your burrows on the brink of the desert, where no water can be reached and where your babes may dehydrate in the wretched dust, for all I care."

"Your opinions coincide so effortlessly with the ideology of Shimnon the Elder," said Zander, "one of history's most renowned bigots and instigators of hate. Allow me to guess—he's one of your favorite authors, right?"

"My ideas are entirely my own. Any coincidence of sentiment, it should go without saying, is not intentional unless the grounds for its establishment be that of reason."

"You do know why we are up in arms, don't you?"

"No. I haven't a clue."

"Sunflower Country's population has, over the past few years, more than tripled. Where once less than a thousand Mice coexisted between the Two Rivers, now nearly four thousand are struggling in an area the same size as that which our founders discovered so long ago. Surrounding lands are uninhabitable, mostly desert and Snake-infested forest, and while the more affluent class now owns the majority of livable property, the poor and underprivileged are left with the dirty corners, dusty dunes, and rocky slopes of land. The situation is not only unfair, it is perversely unjust. Something must be done about it soon, before a civil war erupts."

"But tell me this, Zander—do the poor deserve to live on the choice plots of land? What have they done to earn that right?"

"We Bums are adamantly opposed to labor of any kind, but we are Mice just like you, and deserve all the accoutrements of the wealthy. All I am saying is simply this: we are done bowing in obedience to our oppressors, done are we with the business of supplicating the rich and powerful, and we are through with living with the crust, while others consume daily the heart of the bread. Infinite Expansionalism is only possible when one can expand infinitely, but the limited nature of our resources, accompanied by a burgeoning population, can mean only one thing—we must resort to Bummunism to save the world."

"Who will gather kernels? Who will look out for Snakes? Who will perform the many duties of Government?"

"We each would gather our own. It is futile to look out for Snakes. And most of Government is a ridiculous waste of time."

This conversation might have continued indefinitely, with Zander and myself having our backs to the bars, sitting side-by-side and damned with each other's presence, but alas it was not to be. We heard a distant rumbling and the ground shook beneath us. Twigs were snapping loudly and bushes were literally being tossed aside. Something enormous, probably a Man, was on the way.

"Damn you and your Bummunist ways!" I cursed Zander. "Look what you've done to us now!"

"Relax," said Zander, "it's not so bad."

"Have you been caught before?" I asked.

In answer, Zander just smiled. It became apparent to me then that he had had some experience in the past with these Humans, which he was not willing to share with me for, no doubt, some vile and heinous reason. I cast a silent prayer to One Paw to spare my life in this, my dire time of need.

"What are you going to do if you escape?" asked Zander. "Go back to your office and pretend to make weighty decisions?"

"I would have you know, the decisions I pretend to make are of the utmost importance to the Mice of my country." The noise steadily grew louder, until we were able to discern the heavy thud of footsteps.

"But isn't it just like you and your kind to beat around the bush and accomplish next to nothing in the good and valuable time that One Eye has granted us?"

"What I do in Government reveals a cautiousness that is clearly rational; what you profess to know about the workings of Government reveals an ignorance that is clearly absurd. Dare you question my authority?"

"You," he rebuked, "are an incompetent wretch!"

"And you," I barked in return, "are an uneducated, unenlightened, brainless and heartless piece of worthless, short-tailed—" A man's oversized hand picked the cage up roughly from one end and, as we two Mice, deviating in our opinions, conflicting in our beliefs, tumbled across each other to the lower end, I concluded my stream of epithets with a single, squealed syllable: "—*scum!*"

The man reached into our wiry abode and made as if to grab my accomplice in this terrifying experience. Zander, for what it was worth, dodged this way and that, clambering across me and digging his claws painfully into my fur coat, squealing with a Female Mouse's uninhibited fright. But alas, his struggle was ineffectual! The man merely squeezed him all the tighter for his efforts, until at last he lost his breath, being constricted so violently in this manner.

I knew that Man was far and away the most dangerous of all our predators but, for some reason or other, found myself less afraid of this creature than I had been of the slimy, fork-tongued, Mouse-devouring Snake. Consequently, I did not resist when the Man's hands came groping in the cage for me, accompanied by the thunderous vocalization: "*Oh my! What have we here? Another one, and fancy—in the same trap! Luck is with me today!*"

I was flung haphazardly into some large cloth bag and a darkness, impenetrable and complete, overwhelmed me. The pitiable wait for my own demise had begun.

THE LABYRINTH

When I awoke, my vision was blurred, and the fuzzy gray objects I saw wavering before my eyes instinct alone told me were my very own paws. Slowly, sight returned to me. I sat on my haunches as still as possible until such time as I could better discern my surroundings. My nose told me, when I sniffed the sterilized ammonia in the air, that I was in a Man-Lab, and this knowledge alone was adequate enough to suffuse my body with terror and freeze my limbs in shock. A voice, timid and distant, reached me in my disabled state.

"Hallo," it said. I began to think that perhaps I was deluded, or suffering an auditory hallucination of some sort. Then it recurred: "Halloooooooo! You there, what's your name, sir? It pleaseth good Hamrick to know your name."

"Percy," I responded, in a breathless whisper.

"What? What was that?"

I grunted and groaned from the effort to make myself louder, and pronounced at length much more clearly the second time around, "Percy! I am Percy of the land between the Two Rivers. I alone am leader of Sunflower Country, making decisions that require further decisions, endlessly so. These decisions have an effect, or lack thereof, upon over four thousand discontented Mice."

Haughty laughter ensued. "This Mouse is ridiculous!" I heard one say. Another booming voice from behind piped in with, "We have a wild one here." Yet another said, "His entire life is senseless!" And still another said, "Be gentle with the newcomers, boys."

"My life is not ridiculous or senseless," I returned, "nor am I in any way wild, but entirely civilized, and educated in the liberal arts college of Sunflower Country. I am not a newcomer either, but twelve-years-old on the earth today."

More laughter, which continued uninterrupted for several moments, followed this statement.

"Don't talk to them," said Zander, whose voice emanated from somewhere behind me. I turned to greet him, happy that I was not in this boat alone.

"Well, it's good to see you. I never thought I'd say that."

"They are tamed Mice and Laboratory Rats, untrained in the art of civility, ignorant of nations and Governments and Presidents, and wholly without manners, the most hideous and useless creatures in One Eye's world."

My vision was now fully recovered, and so I turned about in a slow circle, gathering thereby a crude appraisal of my environment. The first thing that came to my attention was the fact that I was locked inside another cage, this one a flimsily built aluminum piece that was just strong enough to hold me, and no stronger. The next was that I was surrounded on all sides, and above and below, by other cages, filled with other Mice, as well as creatures that looked like us, but were four times larger. The offal stench of feces was ever-present in my senses and made me feel nauseous. In the cage to my immediate left there sat Zander, seemingly unperturbed by the commotion of his neighbors or by the flagrant assault on his senses.

"Where are we?" I asked him.

"In a Man-Lab, where else?" he returned sarcastically, waving his paws about him as if the explanation were self-evident.

A small, blindingly white Mouse in the cage to my right spoke to me, and I recognized his voice from the earlier conversation: "Good Hamrick knoweth your name now, but he has never heard of Sunflower Country. What place is this? How did you escape from your cage?"

"Oh shut up!" said Zander, "For crying out loud, you dumb Mouse!"

"Good Hamrick, if it pleaseth, knoweth why you are here, and what fate may befall you."

As Zander did not take the opportunity right away to respond to this, I ventured a question, desiring to learn as much about my new whereabouts as was possible. "Why are we here, good Hamrick, and what fate awaits us?"

"You are here because the Man named Peter desireth to run some experiments upon you which you may or may not survive. Your fate rests on your ability to fulfill His demands efficiently and with great vigor. He will pit the two of you against each other in a dreadful contest of strength and cunning. The winner wins, and walks away unharmed. The loser loses, and dies."

"How do you know this?" I asked.

"Because that is what he does. Always. Experiments and needles and knives and horrible smells—*oh the smells!* It is enough to drive a Mouse insane. Many of us here have long since lost our minds. I recognize your friend there. Zander, is it? He's been here before, and won."

"Is that so?" I asked, turning my attention back to Zander.

"The white one lies!" he hissed. "Never have I stepped foot in these sterile quarters!"

"Good Hamrick never forgetteth a face," said Hamrick, speaking of himself in the third person.

"I've never been here before!" cried Zander.

"You have, I'll wager my white coat to that," Hamrick persisted in his accusation, heedless of my accomplice's feelings.

"Well, well, well," I said, looking directly in Zander's eyes. "We're just full of surprises today, aren't we?"

"You believe this filthy trash? You would take his word over mine? I tell you, I have never been here before."

"Whom did ye kill?" said Hamrick. "Was it the small Mouse that you outwitted in the labyrinth? Yes, 'twas the labyrinth, 'twasn't it? Killed him, ye did, and heartlessly so, if recollection serveth correctly."

"Liar!" screamed Zander, but I suspected that it was he who withheld the truth.

The conversation desisted almost at once as a rush of wind accompanied the opening and closing of the Lab's door, and the Man came waltzing in humming a tune, all decked out in a long white jacket. A sudden terror of enormous proportions seized me. I thought that there, in that Man, could be seen the face of death, without expression or emotion or concern. He was a calculated killer. He knew what he was doing. He measured his massacres in teaspoons and quarts, ounces and inches—the scientific way—and nothing that I could have done or said would have excused me from the challenge that lay before me. I would be pitted against Zander in a contest of strength and cunning, and the winner would live, and the loser die.

And Zander had experience in this business that gave him the clear advantage going into it.

"You hate me, don't you?" I asked him.

Zander appeared to contemplate this suggestion seriously for a moment, before turning to me with a look of extraordinary sadness in his long, hirsute face. "I don't want to kill you, Percy. I think that perhaps if circumstances had been different, you and I could have been friends. But the Man…you see, the Man brings out the evil in us. It's every Mouse for himself out there. Don't you get it? I'm not going to do anything to help you once the competition begins."

My unfriendly abode rattled violently and appeared to be coming apart at the hinges. It was then that I realized I was moving—and Zander in his cage alongside me—floating through the air and swinging back and forth. I was still in the cage, but the illusion that I was flying was convincing enough to make me sick to my stomach. The smell was overpowering, and I tweaked my nose between my claws to shut it out. At last the Man settled us in our separate cages high above the floor, which looked impenetrable, and on a counter that was long and black and filled with vials and medical paraphernalia. I could not even guess at the use of each of the strange things I saw. Speaking truthfully, I did not want to know.

The Man whistled and hummed to himself constantly. It seemed an habitual practice when he was alone in the room with us. Zander and I kept our silence all this while, but watched in fascination and growing alarm as he prepared two syringes, first by removing some protective outer cap, then by plunging the needle into a vial of clear fluid, and finally by depressing the plunger and drawing it back, filling it to a certain, measured point and placing it aside while he did this same procedure once more. Two syringes—one for me, one for Zander.

In my cage, I cowered in the corner with my paws over my head, and in his cage, Zander ran around in frantic little circles—both of us equally helpless.

The Man's gigantic hand, protected in a plastic glove, came probing inside the cage, reaching out for me. He settled upon me in my corner. I was tightly squeezed and hefted out of an opening in the top of the cage, one that I had not previously known existed.

Then came a sudden pinch in my rear that I assumed must have been the syringe biting me. The Man set me down on the counter and I rushed to its edge—only to peer over and down, what seemed like miles away, where the hard, ceramic floor awaited my fall. I cringed and froze there on the precipice, sniffed the air, and turned back around to face the Man and his now-empty syringe.

He was laughing at me.

"*Go ahead and jump, little one!*" He laughed some more, mocking my predicament. "*Although I dare say, that floor might hurt.*"

I did not know what he thought I was capable of. But I was a brave enough Mouse, and I could make decisions when somebody forced my paw. My priorities were simple: the Man would kill me for sure; the floor *might* kill me. So in the end there really was no decision to make. But suddenly I was feeling very dizzy. The world began to spin in my perception. I could feel that medicine he injected in me running its dreadful course.

Whether I jumped or simply fell is beyond my exact recollection. The next thing I knew, I was on the floor and could barely move, not because I was hurt in any way—the fall, surprisingly enough, did not hurt me—but because the medicine was having its deleterious and numbing effect on my limbs. I wondered briefly the cause behind the Man's decision to drug me.

The Man picked me up again, stroking my back with his thumb. *"Christ, little one! You're a brave one, indeed. I've never had a Mouse do that before. Are you all right?"*

Of course I could not have answered him, and I'm not sure if I had that he would have understood me. I wanted to tell him that I was Percy, President of Sunflower Country, that I was an important Mouse and that, as such, he was not permitted to perform his experiments on me. Upon any of my subjects perhaps it would be permissible, but not me. But he was already through with consoling words and, before I knew what was happening to me, I was thrust bodily into a large wooden box with a long wooden corridor. The smell of cheese, vague and distant, crept into my senses. I started towards it, and the next thing I knew, I was running headlong down the corridor, the growling vacancy in my stomach propelling my little feet, turning left, then right, then back left again, in what could only have been some sort of merciless labyrinth.

I took several wrong turns, but it was a simple enough matter to get back on the right track. I scurried as fast as I could, realizing as I did so that the speed with which I accomplished this task might be measured against Zander's. After what seemed like an eternity, I made it around the last bend and sprinted down a long straightaway. My olfactory sense told me that the cheese was right around the corner.

And yes, there it was. But before I could satisfy my cravings for food, I was snatched up out of the labyrinth, and the Man announced so that all could hear, *"Twenty-two seconds and thirteen hundredths of a second."*

I was thrust roughly back in my cage at about the same time that Zander was retrieved. The same ritual was carried out with the syringe, only this time Zander had the presence of mind not to jump from that absurd height. Moments later, he was put in the wooden labyrinth and began running almost immediately. I realized that I was able to see his every movement, and that if he had been able to see me as I was seeing him, he had yet another advantage over me in knowing just what route to take ahead of time.

When it was all over, the Man announced, "*Nineteen seconds and sixty-seven hundredths of a second.*" Then he lifted Zander up in the air and his voice boomed around the room, "*You're our lucky winner in the labyrinth!*" Then he thrust Zander back in his cage, put our separate cages back on the shelf with the other creatures, fiddled with a few of his vials on the long, black counter and left the room, turning off the light as he did so.

I heard the voice of Hamrick beside me: "Don't worry, Percy. You'll get your chance. There are more events to come."

I fell over on my side and lost consciousness.

THE DREAM

At first the dream seemed so real that I was not able to distinguish it from reality. "I am a Bummunist," said a Female voice to me from far, far away, "and a Blue also." "Who are you?" I asked. "You'll find out soon enough, Percy."

I began to see before me a long stretch of sand, empty and forlorn. The desert, in all my reckonings, looked just like this. I was not afraid, however, but merely pleased to have escaped from the Man-Laboratory. "Where am I?" I asked, directing my question all about me, for I did not know whence the voice originated.

"In the Drylands, the home of all Blues."

I gasped and thought to myself, 'Well then, I am not at all that far from home, am I?' Aloud, I said again, "Who are you? The voice sounds terribly familiar."

"You'll find out soon enough, Percy."

"Where are all the Blues, if this is their home?" I asked.

"Keep walking, and you will see."

I walked on, my claws sinking into the loose sand with each hesitant step. A sudden thirst overwhelmed me. And a strong desire to urinate. I resisted my cravings and impulses with as much will power as I could muster, and concentrated solely on putting one paw before the other in my slow, monotonous movement across the hot sand. "Are you still there?" I asked. "I do not want to be alone."

The voice responded, "I am still here. I am not going anywhere until you have learned your lesson."

"And what lesson is that?" I asked.

"All things will be revealed to you in good time, Percy. Be patient, and continue walking. Any direction will do."

I stopped walking momentarily and looked around me. Any direction? There was nothing but sand as far as the eye could see in every direction. The voice prodded me onward, "Perhaps you need a little incentive."

"What do you mean by that?" I asked.

"You are just full of questions today, aren't you? Quick, look behind you!" I turned around and beheld in the distance a horrific sight: the Man was approaching fast with a syringe in one hand, a cage in the other. "He's coming for you, Percy! Run!"

I turned tail and scampered as fast as I could through the hot sand, the injunction that 'any direction will do' still fresh in my mind. 'What am I to learn from this?' I thought. 'That Man is the most dangerous animal on the planet?' I already knew that. Perhaps some further lesson was to be realized. As if in answer to my thoughts, the voice met my ears, "You will learn the grave error of your ways, and what fate you may experience in the near future if you are not careful." Needless to say, I had not previously suspected any grave error in my ways and consequently considered that perhaps I was dreaming, after all. Perhaps this, this terror-laden occurrence, was but the manifestation of my imagination in what could have been nothing less than a full-fledged nightmare. A Man was chasing me, the conditions of sand and heat were unbearable, and a strange

Mousette voice was consulting with me about my fate. I did not believe in fate, or anything supernatural for that matter, but it was something of a rude awakening to realize that a voice was descending all around me from everywhere and nowhere at once. Regardless of the thoughts that kept coursing through my head, I continued running as fast as possible, desiring not to go back in that damned cage.

I ran and ran and ran, but when at last it seemed my feet could carry me no farther, I collapsed on the sand and waited for the Man's hand to squeeze me. After a good spell, when no hand found me, I considered that I must have lost the heathen who was chasing me and, in light of my good fortune, I whooped and hollered triumphantly.

"It's not over yet," came the voice. "Get up, and continue walking." Despite the sheer physical exhaustion that I felt, I obeyed this command willingly and immediately, rather than lie there in that burning sand.

Only a few minutes later I came upon a cliff face peppered with burrow holes. I thanked One Paw above and climbed up to the first of these retreats in the sand. Darting quickly inside the burrow— the better to get out of the sun—I called out to the inhabitants in my loudest, most booming voice, and in the deathly quiet that came back to me, there could be heard nothing but my own hoarse breathing and the sound of my heart thudding against my rib cage.

"Where am I?" I asked the lady. "You are in the burrow of Urlap, a Bummunist and a Blue like myself, who passed on not too long ago, during the great extermination."

"Genocide?" I asked.

"Something like that."

"I am not an advocate of genocide," I said.

"Oh, but you are just a step or two away from vanquishing all Bummunists and Blues."

"That's not true!" I cried.

I waddled deeper into the cave, turning several corners and following my nose. At length I reached a bedroom, and there in the dust—for there were no cedar shavings such as could be found in the heart of the country amongst the Greens—I beheld a wretched sight, and it made me want to puke.

Three Mice, Blue in nature, all of them without any perception of life, were huddled together in the corner, their bodies appearing totally emaciated, so much so that I could count the ribs. I witnessed white, grotesque worms—maggots!—crawling out of apertures in their sides. Fear and disgust arrested me. For several seconds, I could not move.

When finally I was able to break free, I scurried out the hole as fast as my little legs would carry me and flung myself headlong back into the sand. I threw up a mixture of bile and something green. At last, recovering my voice, I asked the lady, "Who did this?"

"You did."

"Speak honestly, Mousette, who did this? I'll not hold it against you!"

"Perhaps if I had done it, you would be well served to hold it against me. But I did not. You alone are responsible for the death of these good Mice. Remember the words of Shimnon: You will know him when he comes—Scampering like the sun across the sky—An enemy to all Blues and Bums. *That is the Mouse on the Mountain. That is you, Percy."*

"I am responsible for this?" I pleaded. "Impossible…" I contemplated my own wretchedness for several moments, my immorality in the eyes of One Paw, and came at last to the realization that I was an evil Mouse, unfit to live.

"This has not happened yet," said the Female.

"Really! Then how can it be prevented?" I asked.

"The future is not avoidable, Percy, but it is up to you to make the effort to try and amend things with your subjects. Then what would happen to you—therein lies the tragedy, Percy."

"What happens to me?" I asked.

"Close your eyes," she said, and I did so. "Now, open them." When I opened my eyes, I was at the peak of Mount Enex. I looked all about me, and the spectacle was magnificent, truly breathtaking. "That's you," she said. I heard her voice right beside me and turned to look at her.

It was my mother, who had died when I was just a child. Still graceful. Still beautiful in my perception. Still wise and gracious. The one Mouse whom I looked up to more than any other, and whose spirit, time after time, I had wished to come visit me from beyond the grave. "That," she said softly, "that is you. In the pit."

The pit was a small valley in Mount Enex and a place where condemned criminals were sent to live out their last days on earth. I saw myself in the pit, a deplorable sight, scratching frantically away on some medium of paper. "I'm going to die like this, Mother?"

"You are on only one condition—that you try to save the Bummunists. You are not obligated to do so, however. Be wise and just, Percy. Do what you know in your heart to be the best thing. And remember: I am a Bummunist."

"You? A Bummunist?"

"You were too young to remember, Percy. Too young. Your father knew that when he married me. We never dreamed that our son would grow up to be the Mouse on the Mountain. Look at all that you've accomplished, son. Make us proud." Her voice descended to a whisper. I reached out for her with my paw.

"Make us proud. Make us proud…Percy."

THE CONTEST

The voice of Hamrick roused me from my slumber. "Good Percy," he said, "it pleaseth good Hamrick to talk to you." I rubbed my eyes nonchalantly and looked around me. Zander and his cage were nowhere to be seen, but there was Hamrick, like a permanent fixture in my new landscape, right beside me. The lights to the Laboratory were on.

"What?" I replied groggily.

"It pleaseth good Hamrick—"

"I know that much, Hamrick! What do you want to talk about?"

"The contest."

"What about it?" I said.

"Even though you lost the first event, there still be some hope for you. The second event is distance running, and the third is new to all of us, but involves water and something of a swim. Dost thou swimmeth, good Percy?"

"I am a fair swimmer, yes," I said, though in truth I had not waddled in water since I was a young Mousekin.

"Well, if you're no good at distance running, it might help that you can swim. Can your friend, Zander, swim?"

"I don't know," I answered, exasperated by this discourse. "Why am I here?" I asked. "Why does he need us when he has you and the rest of your kind?"

"The Man, Peter, liketh to run experiments on wild Mice as well, and to compare the results against those of Laboratory Mice such as I. He does the same thing with Rats. We do not pretend to understand all that goes through the Man's mind. We just do as he says and, for the most part, ask no questions."

"Where is Zander?"

"Your friend got taken away while you were sleeping. I do not know why or where."

A rumbling, deep voice from beneath me spoke up through the cages. "He godda taken to tha treadmill for a lit'l jog 'n' a lit'l 'lectrokyushion." I looked down and saw a gigantic Rat peering up through the bars at me. "My name Lars. I be a—a Rat!"

"So I see. Tell me, Lars—has the contest recommenced in my slumber?"

"That't as, yes!"

"What is *'lectrokyushion*?"

"Ah! Pain, p-p-p-p-paaaaaaaaaain!"

"What is he talking about, Hamrick?"

"Lars sayeth that electrocution is pain. The paw of evil hath created it, for the purpose of tormenting all the little creatures of the world. You will knoweth it when you feel it, and not before time, and you will feeleth it when you stop running, and not before time; therefore it be useless to describe it."

"Man makes it so that it seems we are killing one another," I said.

"That be so."

"Oh, foul prison from damnation! Begone! Let me alone! Leave me be! Let me go free! Oh, how I hate Man and all his evil machinations! What does he think I am, some kind of guinea pig? Alas, the guinea pigs are treated unjustly also, and I am not in the least surprised!"

"There be little use in getting excited," said Hamrick. "You may be the President of over four thousand Mice in Sunflower Country, but you have no power here, Percy. All fate rests in the paws of your enemy—Man."

Suddenly, in the distance I heard a cry, a prolonged and pain-filled wailing that I knew came from Zander, but was not willing to believe it. Then I heard the voice of the Man, as he announced so all could hear, "*Thirty-two minutes, fifty-four seconds, and twenty-six hundredths of a second! Good for you, little one! That's a new record!*"

Before long, Zander's cage rattled back in place beside mine and I had a moment to witness a pitiable sight: Zander was laid out on his back, panting heavily and crying, the tears coursing down his hairy cheeks liberally and without a care as to where they would wind up. He turned over slowly and looked at me, and I saw that his eyes were bloody. There was blood also coming from somewhere on his tail. "Good luck, Percy!" he exclaimed breathlessly.

I had no time to respond, for just then the Man's hand gripped me in its iron-like vice and I was escorted bodily to the treadmill, a long, inclined conveyer belt divided into ten sections by transparent glass so that ten Mice or Rats could run side-by-side. I was more afraid of 'electrocution' than I was of death, and in fact, I prayed for death as I hung suspended in midair in the Man's hand. All I could do was wait, but One Paw received more desperate prayers in those few moments than He had received in all His existence. I vowed that I would become more religious if ever I got out of this alive. But what were the chances of that? Thirty-two minutes and fifty-four seconds and twenty-six hundredths of a second would be impossible for an old Mouse such as myself to best. Damn that Zander! No, on second thought, damn the Man for pitting us against each other so ruthlessly!

I was put on the treadmill and the belt beneath me started to move. I saw a series of metal bars at the foot of the cage—the source of the electrocution, no doubt. I had no choice but to run.

So, run I did.

The speed with which the belt moved beneath me gradually increased with time, and before long I was sweating and breathing hard. I concentrated on all the good Mice of my country, pondering what they would possibly do without me as their leader. How could they carry on without me? The Mice of Sunflower Country, the land between the Two Rivers, needed me, didn't they?

Suddenly I realized that they did not, and this realization caused me to stumble. I came dangerously close to the bars at the bottom of the treadmill. Was I expendable? I understood then, in a moment of clarity afforded me by the fact that my life was flashing before my eyes, that I was. The Mice of my country did not need me. I was a useless Mouse in all respects. My only strength was my ability to snow everyone who took the time to listen to me.

'My life is far from over,' I pledged. 'If ever I get back to Sunflower Country, I shall resume my position as President and see to it that the Mice of my glorious homeland get all that they deserve.'

After that, I was too tired to think, but the image of my Mother was ever-present in my mind. I ran for her, and for every Mouse that wished for something he did not get. I ran for One Paw, and for Zander, for Hamrick and Lars, for Chipper and Harold, for Teddy and Bobby, for Neil and Oliver, for Niner, my best friend, and even for old Tessa, my wife. I ran and ran and ran, until I could run no more, and slid down to the dreaded bars of electrocution. At first nothing happened, and I sat on the bars expectant of some great pain.

Then I felt it, a sharp stinging sensation that brought tears to my eyes and caused my nose to begin pouring out a profusion of blood. I jumped back on the conveyer belt, more compelled to do so than not, and continued running. But it was not long before I gave out again. This time I thought that no amount of electrocution could get me going again, but I was wrong. I ran and ran some more. Finally, my limbs refused to move anymore, and I wound up on the bars getting shocked again and again.

At last, the Man turned his wicked machine off, and as he picked me up announced so all could hear, "*Twenty-nine minutes and fifty-six seconds and eighty-four hundredths of a second.*"

I had lost again.

I tumbled back into my cage, hurting terribly from my exertions, and from the electric shocks. But we were allowed no rest, and Zander, in his near-comatose state was rudely jerked forth by the Man, who said as he left, "*Time for a swim, little one.*"

I heard Zander scream, "I cannot swim! I cannot swim!" His voice faded into the walls, the sharp corners and sterilized surfaces of the terrorizing Laboratory.

I was too exhausted to follow Zander's progress anymore, but Hamrick was watching the whole thing, and gave startling commentary, "Ah, there he goes, into the water. Dear me, he hath sunk straightaway to the bottom of the tub. He's not coming up! He's not coming up! Help him, Peter! Help him! Ah, there he goes again, he finally hath surfaced! There you go, Zander-boy. There you go. Ah, he's sinking again. This goeth not well for the lad. I don't think he is going to make it. Percy! Percy, you've got a chance, my friend! All you have to do is—"

"Shut up," I said.

"Excuse me?"

"Shut up."

"But I was only trying to—"

"I said, shut…up!" This anger and growing disgust that had been welling up inside my soul had finally reached a breaking point. I could not take this anymore. I refused to participate in murder, even if my accomplice was more than willing to play along. You have a choice to make, Percy: sink or swim, die or kill. What's it going to be, old boy?

The Man paused before Zander's cage, holding the poor Mouse aloft. Zander appeared now, for all his former virility, like a wet and dissolute, tired and bloody mass of fur. "*I'm disappointed in you, little one,*" said the Man, with calculated indifference. "*I thought for sure you'd be the one.*" Then with an "*Ah, well,*" he threw Zander head over feet into his cage, and reached with his other hand into mine.

I had more energy than Zander going into the final event, because I had not completely worn myself out on the treadmill, but I was still physically exhausted and did not think myself capable of staying afloat. 'We shall find out soon enough,' I thought. The Man had me by the scruff of my neck, painfully pinching my fur between thumb and forefinger.

Moments later, I was tossed into a small tub and, swallowing a good deal of water on the way, I sank directly to the bottom. I kicked and thrashed until I made it to the surface again. Looking around me, I discovered in the distance a beach of sand. I decided to make for this beach. It seemed like the sensible thing to do, given the fact that I had not been afforded any specific directions concerning how to play this game.

I kicked with my legs, stroked with my paws, and paddled in the only way I knew how. The thought that I might be killing my accomplice, I confess, did not even occur to me while I was in that tub of water.

Eventually I staggered out onto the beach and fell promptly to the sand. I could not have moved another inch.

The Man picked me up again and loudly declared, "*You are the winner!*" I was taken back to my cage, however, and hurled within. I curled up in a corner trying to get warm, but there were no cedar shavings in there. Hamrick tried to talk with me, and I found to my surprise that conversation with the white Mouse would not at all be disagreeable to me.

"You've won, Percy. Thou shalt walketh free. You are getting out of here for good. Oh, how I wish our situations were reversed! But I must stay in this cage forever, or at least until the day I die."

The reality of this knowledge—the knowledge that I would be free again—did not make an immediate impression on me. I asked Hamrick, "And what is to happen to Zander?"

"Sticketh around and see."

"Stop talking about me like I'm not here," came the voice of Zander behind me.

"Sorry, Zander."

"I'll tell you what's going to happen to me, Percy. I'm going to die now. My entire life will have been for nothing, without purpose, without consequence. I am dead, and you are alive."

"No," I said frantically. "Maybe we can escape."

"There is no escape from the dungeons of Man."

"We've got to continue hoping, Zander."

"There is no hope for or against Man."

"But, we—"

"All is lost, Percy."

"All is not lost!" I countered, suddenly furious. "You will be remembered, Zander! I shall travel to the Drylands and visit your kind! I shall spread the word that you died for a cause—the cause of freedom for all Mice! I shall tell them that you sacrificed yourself for the betterment of the general public! You will be worshipped in Sunflower Country as a martyr of the highest order!"

I did not realize that I was pacing fretfully about the cage while speaking until Zander told me to desist at once.

"If you do travel to the Drylands, and for some reason I doubt that you will, just tell my brothers and sisters that I love them, that I shall always love them even from beyond death. Love is eternal, Percy. It is the only thing that lasts forever."

The Man's hand swung aside the latch to Zander's cage, lifted the gate, and reached inside for the poor, helpless victim of his underhanded machinations. Zander scampered quickly away from the hand, but all his efforts were, in the end, futile. He panicked and called out to me one last time as the fingers of the Man closed about him: "*Tell them I love them, Percy! Tell them I love them!*"

"You will not be forgotten!" I cried.

"*Tell them…*"

THE DRYLANDS

I shall not torment you with the more horrifying details of Zander's demise. My conscience does not permit a description of this variety, if only because I myself was partially responsible for the poor Blue's death. Let it suffice that his manner of end closely resembled in every aspect the killings in my former dreams. At my paws and the hands of an evil Man did he pass away, but I vowed again and again that he would live on. The Mice of Sunflower Country would remember their fallen hero.

Because I am running short on time here, I shall relate to you no more of my experience in the Laboratory. The Man released me into the wild, in a desert that was not dissimilar to the one I had dreamt of, and from there the story will continue.

I wandered about hopelessly the entire first day of my newfound freedom and, unfortunately, appeared to make no progress. For all I could tell, I was drifting around in circles, dying from the heat and profound thirst. To make matters worse, the Man had attached some sort of plastic tag to my left ankle, and now it scraped in the sand behind me, leaving a trail not unlike that of a Snake. I was disheartened not only on account of the weather, which was dreadfully hot and dry, but also because I had lost a comrade in the Lab, and nothing I could do, no amount of beseeching to One Paw or One Eye, no amount of legislation which might pass under the guidance of my claws, would be sufficient to bring him back. In a fit of delirium, I found myself sympathetic to the plight of all Bummunists and fancied that I would set aright all the injustices that they had been dealt under my supervision. Thinking such wild thoughts, it occurred to me at last that I would not be capable of this manner of vindication, for soon enough I would be as dead as Zander, and wholly unfit thereby to lead a country. Despite my frustrations and acute sense of futility, I somehow made it to nightfall, and was able to curl up in a hole in the sand and fall sleep without further discomfort. The next day I awoke to the sun glaring in my eyes, and the heat, already oppressive, seemed to push down upon me from above like a great weight, like the palm of a Man's hand in which was situated a devouring flame. I was dehydrated and desperate. I needed water. I did not know where I was. Something compelled me to get up and start moving again, that something being the memory of Zander. I wandered on and on and tried to keep in the same bearing, though how successful I was at this would be anyone's guess. I heard the voice of Hamrick in my mind: "Thou wouldst die, Percy, after all that ye have been through?" Then Niner: "Welcome to the land of the dead. You can join Zander and me over here. What do you think of that, Percy? What do you think of that, eh?" Then finally, Mother: "Stay true to your heart, son. Stay true to your soul."

I know not when I lost consciousness, but when I awoke I was no longer in the sun, but on the floor of someone's burrow. I half choked as that someone threw water on my face, the better to awaken me. "Huh! Wha! Where am I?" I said, having regained my senses.

"You are in Sunflower Country, One Eye's most damned nation in all the world."

I breathed a sigh of relief, "Then take me to my comrades in the Senate Burrow, for I am none other than Percy, President of Sunflower Country."

"Are you now? President Percy disappeared with Zander over a month ago. None have seen hide or hair of either of them since. Both are assumed dead."

"I tell the truth," I insisted. "I am Percy, and I was with Zander when he died, at the hands of a Man in a Laboratory far, far away from here. In whose burrow am I currently residing? With whom do I presently speak?"

"My name is Grunt. I am the son of Urlap."

The name sent chills down my spine. I had heard that name before, and it was in the dream with my Mother. Urlap had been the Mouse whose entire family I had seen crawling with worms as they decayed in their burrow. So stunned was I at this newfound knowledge that I could only remark, without energy, "You and your family are Bummunists, aren't you?"

"That we are," said Grunt, not without a little hostility in his voice. "If you *are* Percy, *the* Mouse on the Mountain, and you're responsible for the death of Zander, you came to the wrong place, mister."

"No, you don't understand. I'm not responsible..." My voice faded as I realized the untruth that I had been about to speak. In a previous lifetime I could have spoken this lie with incredible ease, and gotten away with it. But now some sense of guilt overwhelmed me and I bit my tongue back in disgust.

"You're not responsible?" asked Grunt.

"No, I—I meant yes—in a way," I stammered.

A large Mouse stepped into the room, which was no more than a hole in the dirt, and spoke to me in a loud, booming voice: "My name is Urlap." Turning to Grunt, he said, "You are excused, son." Grunt scuffled out of the room, and the Mouse named Urlap continued. "Who are you, and what were you doing in the Drylands this time of year? You almost died out there, fool!"

"I am Percy, the President of Sunflower Country, and I had just been set free by a Man who had me imprisoned in a hideous Laboratory. The Mouse you know as Zander was with me, but fell prey to an unfortunate end, while I was somehow permitted to take leave of the confines of that terrible prison."

"Why am I to believe you? Prove yourself."

"Zander kidnapped me on the day of my wedding, when I was to be married to a Mousette named Tessa, and took me to the southern edge of Fern Valley, where we immersed ourselves into the thickets, a tack to my throat all the while. We stumbled into a Man cage and would have been saved, but the Mouse named Darian, trying to help us, was devoured by a Snake, while we witnessed the entire bloody affair from safety within the cage. Then the Man came and took us to his white Laboratory, where we met several other Mice, equally white, who had nothing of existence but to sit in their cages and do the Man's bidding. We were forced to compete against each other in those dreaded environs, first meandering through a labyrinth, then running on a treadmill for distance and time, and finally swimming in a basin of water. At the last of these events, Zander was ill fated and nearly drowned. Though he bested me in the first two exercises, my victory in the third sealed his doom. The Man Peter took Zander away and massacred him, setting me free in the desert to fend for myself against the sun."

Urlap maintained a silence for some time, as if contemplating all that I had said and pondering whether or not I told the truth. At last, he spoke, "Your story is outrageous, and hardly believable for a Mouse, but you speak true to the politician's manner of conversing, and so I am inclined to trust that you speak either a tale so tall it reaches the canopy of the highest forest, or merely the truth, though that is hard to imagine coming from your kind. However, it is apparent to me from your discourse that you are responsible for the death of our leader. Therefore, you must die."

"Wait!" I cried. "He told me to tell you all something!"

"What is that?"

"He told me to tell you that he loved you, and would always, from even beyond the grave. He has, furthermore, inspired me to take action in favor of my would-be enemies, the Blues and Bummunists of Sunflower Country, when I have reestablished my power and regained my office, so that all of the injustices you have suffered at the paws of the Greens may be absolved."

Urlap scratched his chin in contemplation. His wife came up behind him and draped her arms around his neck. "We must let him go," she said. "He is on our side, Urlap."

"Yes, but he killed Zander!"

"But he has a wounded conscience, can't you see, and is willing to set things aright again, for us and our kind."

In my mind, I thanked this Female Mouse graciously, and thus was my decision to help the Blues reaffirmed. I owed my life to them now, and to Zander. My life no longer belonged to me, therefore I was not at liberty to act or speak in my own partiality anymore. The old days, where I could easily compromise my soul and disposition with a word here or a word there, a lie or a pawshake or a batting of my eyelashes, were long over. I was a new Mouse.

"If we let you go, what will you do for us?" asked Urlap.

"I shall personally see to it that you are treated with equal deference under One Eye's expansive sky. No longer will you be relegated to the corners of society, no longer will you suffer in your hot, sandy burrows in the Drylands. Your lot in life will be fairly acquired and justly regarded."

As I said these words, I felt a purity fall over me that I had not felt before, and I knew then that I was doing the right thing, that I was doing what, in my heart, I felt was true. Mother would have been proud.

"Then come, good Percy, and we shall see you on your way. You're welcome in my home anytime." Urlap grabbed me by the shoulder and led me out, but not back into the sun, for it was dark outside and the stars were sprinkled in the heavens in a beautiful and exotic manner that I had never witnessed before.

BACK AGAIN

I scampered up to Niner's burrow.

It was still the dead of night, and I had had to travel under cover of darkness and foliage much of the way through Fern Valley in an attempt to avoid the Snakes and Owls. Fortunately for me, Urlap came much of the way with me, else I would have gotten lost for sure.

"Niner. Niner." I whispered. There was no answer. Losing my patience, I raised my voice and called once more, "Niner!"

"Niner does not live here anymore," came the response, from a Male. "Reveal yourself, burglar, or die at the paws of my Arsenic! I know how to use this stuff!"

"Where is Niner?" I asked.

"Who are you, I say—who are you, or I use it!" I smelled the poison from inside the burrow, and wanted nothing of it, so I gave him my name. "Percy, aye? Are you telling me you are the President, assumed dead now for over a month?"

"That I am."

"I don't believe you. Now, get out of my burrow before I kill you."

"Where is Niner?" I insisted.

"Niner? You mean the Mouse who died two weeks ago from old age?"

"No, I mean the Mouse who lived here before you did."

"That Mouse is dead," said the voice. "I am Ransik. I purchased this property from him before he died. Nobody knows why he passed on. Some say it was a mystery. Others say the Government was involved. I don't know, and I don't care. I just want to go back to sleep, so unless you are going to rob me, Percy, it's best for you to leave."

"Thank you, Ransik." I stepped away. I did not have the capacity to believe that my oldest and best friend was now dead. Mysterious circumstances? The Government involved? What had happened in my absence? The questions circulated throughout my mind, though I could feel little sorrow for the loss of my friend; the reality of his death had not hit me just yet.

I wandered throughout the area for the rest of the night, unable to sleep. At last, just as I was about to collapse from exhaustion, I saw a Mouse, or the shape of one at least, in the hazy distance. Even though it was dark, the stars and moon provided sufficient light for me to make out that this Mouse was hobbling towards me. I was not afraid, for I knew this Mouse, and he was no stranger to me—Bleet!

The old prophet stopped before me. From where I was sitting on the ground, I looked up into his eyes, which seemed to glow blood red, and asked him candidly, "What has happened in my absence, Bleet?"

"You have been assumed dead for over a month now, Percy. I tried to tell everyone that you and Zander were merely suffering at the hands of some evil magician, but nobody would listen to me. Your friend, Harold, has taken control of the Presidency since you left. He has proven a harsh and unyielding leader, wreaking further devastation to the Blues of the land, while in the same breath, selling our most dangerous secrets to foreigners. I fear that our nation is on the verge of collapse; a Revolution is imminent. Soon you will be truly dead, and I shall be glad to join you."

"We may yet avoid catastrophe, Bleet! I shall assume power again, and set the world straight."

"You are not wanted here anymore, Percy. The Mouse who has replaced you, along with all of his accomplices, is not going to be happy to see you again. Look!—already the sun rises in the East. My advice to you, if you are wary of your own skin, is to run and hide."

"I shall not run," I said, standing full up on my haunches, "for I am Percy, President of Sunflower Country, and so shall I be until such time as I am either deposed or dead! I have important business to tend to. Even as the sun rises I am planning my course, and preparing to wrest control back away from Harold."

"You don't want to do that, Percy. They killed Niner for getting in the way, you know. They murdered him in cold blood. He was the victim of shortsighted and political machinations. If you get in their way, they will do the same to you, maybe not tomorrow, or the next day, but soon."

"Thank you for your wisdom, Bleet. You are a good friend. I shall keep in mind what you have said to me this morning, and I shall be wary of my former comrades."

I left Bleet standing there and made my way to the Senate Burrow. It would not be long, I knew, before all of Government set its wheels in motion, and the Senators and Representatives assumed their seats, and the President filled his office. I could not help wondering, as I walked, what had happened to old Tessa. I cared nothing for sex anymore, but I reserved a place in my heart for my wife, and hoped that she had made it all right for herself in my absence. I passed by my old burrow on my left, the university on my right, the library on my left and the park on my right, and continued walking along a direct path to the Senate Burrow, with purpose and vigilance. It seemed just yesterday I had walked this way and passed by a bunch of college students listening to that crazed performer, Twister. Those times, the times of my innocence and ignorance, were so far in my past that I could barely make them out anymore. I had since been transformed from a thoughtless, uncaring, lying and deceiving politician, into a dignified Mouse who lived for a new cause. Never again would I lie, or conceal my emotions, or look down on my fellow Mice, but always would I feel their pain and suffering and try to live alongside them, rather than above them. It was within my means to make a difference in this world, and by One Paw I was ready to do it!

I made my way to what used to be my office, and sat down in my cedar shavings in the corner, waiting for my comrades to come. It was not long before I heard a commotion in the hall, and several Mice approaching. When they reached the door, I heard them stop, and I recognized the voices of Chipper and Harold.

Chipper spoke first, "We must be careful, Harold. An inquisition would not sit well with the Mice of our country, many of whom were born in liberty."

"Either they will believe in One Paw," said Harold, "or they will die. It is not our choice to make."

"Of course, sir."

The door opened and in walked Harold. He did not look up immediately, and so I waited anxiously to communicate with him. I wanted him to see me first, to be confronted rudely with my presence, so that he would know once and for all that I was not dead, that I was back, and prepared to take control of my country again. He paced back and forth in front of the door for several minutes, never once looking up, then at last he turned to look out the window, and his eyes came to rest on me.

"P-P-Percy? Is that you?"

"It is."

"Goodness alive! Percy, it's you!"

"What have you been up to in my absence?"

"Dear me, how did you make it? We all thought you were dead long ago."

"What have you been up to, Harold?" I repeated the question.

"Why, what on earth do you mean? As Vice-President, it was my duty to take over while you were gone. I have been performing in this office for well past a month now."

There passed between us a long and disturbing moment of silence. I was going to leave no doubt as to who was in charge, so I forced him to make the first statement. This statement did not seem immediately forthcoming. I seized his eyes with a cold stare. At length, he relented.

"You can't just come back like this, Percy. We have a thing going on here. We don't need you anymore. You can have your old burrow back, if you like. We'll even find you a wife. But you must have nothing to do with Government again."

"Where is Niner?" I asked. "And Tessa?"

"Tessa had an abortion and, I'm sorry to report, somebody murdered her. Niner passed away from old age. Percy, what are you trying to say, old boy?"

"I want the Presidency back," I said. "I have plans for the Bummunists. They're not as bad as we thought. They have some good ideas about what to do in Government."

"You can't have it," he returned. For the briefest, most frightening of moments, Harold's countenance assumed that of a Man. "The Bummunists are a disgrace to One Paw. Never shall I concede any ground to them while I am in power." He looked at me for a long stretch of time, as if I were some alien whom he did not know anymore, before screaming frantically into the hall, "Guards! Guards! There is an intruder in my office! Come quick, and take him away!"

"I want it back, and I'm going to get it."

"Guards!"

There came a rattling and a hustling down the corridor. Chipper stuck his head in the door and exclaimed in surprise when he saw me. "Percy?"

"This is not Percy," said Harold. "As you know, Percy died several weeks ago. This is an impostor, someone who would claim to be President. He must be put away, at once."

"You won't get away with this!" I shouted to Harold.

Chipper and several guards emerged into the room to arrest me. When my old friend got near, however, in a fit of sudden wrath, I locked my claws into the fur of his body and sank my teeth into his soft throat. "Aggghhhh!" he screamed. At last, after what seemed an eternity, the Police apprehended me.

Chipper's blood covered my coat.

"To the pit! To the pit!" shouted Harold. "He has killed the Vice-President, and must suffer the punishment for murder!"

My head hanging low, and tears pouring from my eyes, I was dragged along in a world that suddenly seemed too languid in my perception, and just for me, when I looked up one last time, Harold, showing all of his yellow teeth, imparted a cruel wink with his left eye.

EPILOGUE

Two days ago, I was sentenced to this damnation, thrust into this deep pit by an ungrateful herd of political rabble-rousers and the new power of Sunflower Country Police, to die alone in the soundless interior of Mount Enex with only my thoughts as companions in a solitude so immense, so absolute, as to be consumptive in its detrimental force, both physically and mentally. This is a challenge, my final challenge, in which I must stay awake for as long as I can to try to relate to you the remainder of my woe-begotten tale. For two days I have suffered in a way unlike any other suffering I have ever experienced, at either the paws of Mice, or the hands of Men. How painful it is to test my stamina in this manner, to make the vain attempt to outlast my hunger and thirst just a little longer, until I can write just a little more, and a little more beyond that.

I consider the possibility that Zander's life was lived in vain, that the Bummunist movement would eventually be crushed and that the rich would continue to tyrannize the poor in Sunflower Country, until such day as a Revolution occurred, and everything was lost, and we would start over from scratch, build upon the same foundation, and reach the same end again, and yet again. History never repeats itself; it mocks itself with similarity. My own life resembles Zander's, that it was lived in vain.

The brittle, weather-hardened bones of the condemned surround me. I wonder what all of these poor Mice were thinking in their final moments of life. I wonder, furthermore, about Chipper, and what fate had befallen him at my paws. My father always told me never to look back on your life with regrets while you are lying on your deathbed. I think how silly and futile it would be for me to fulfill this injunction; for, you see, all my life is one long regret.

Chipper and Zander have now gone to a place where soon enough I shall be joining them. And my country follows closely in our footsteps, collapsing under the momentum of its own self-destruction, cycling downward in a maelstrom of bitter factional rivalry and grave civil unrest.

I sincerely hope that others may learn from our mistakes—or rather, perhaps, from *my* mistakes—for though we be only Mice, and though Mice be not the greatest creatures to roam the earth, yet what we have established here and permitted to fall to ruin was a great and wonderful thing, and if you are guarded in your soul and body, wise and just in your mind, you may see the cause of our misfortune and so one day avoid the same treacherous outcome.

Presently, I feel a weakness spreading throughout my limbs as if I do not have much time left to conclude the tale. I halfheartedly grasp another slip of bubble gum wrapper, a medium that they have been kind enough to afford me in my long hours of solitude, and begin to scratch these final, hurried words. May the heavens preserve all that I have written today.

The stark truth of reality descends upon my soul like a long shadow. Something massive indeed has stepped between the sun and me. I think to myself, 'There is but one choice to make, Percy—either you take the Arsenic and die now, or allow hunger to steal you away later.' Either way, I am dead.

Face-to-face with my own mortality, and with yet another decision to make—alas, how I hate decisions!—I think to myself 'How on earth did you make it here, Percy? And what on earth will you do now?' I suppose if I read my own story I would find answer sufficient for the first of these questions, and time itself will suffice to resolve the latter.

I can speak the name of my country no more. I am lost in shame.

Know that once upon a time there was a Mouse, who was called Percy, and was once esteemed the good title "Mouse on the Mountain," though now is reduced in status to merely a *mouse on the mountain,* and herein his story be told, to what degree truthfully only the Reader may tell.

I put down my paper and reach out with a frail old paw for the poison.